Bulbul Sharma, best selling writer, painter, birdwatcher and maker of woodcuts, is the author of the enormously popular *My Sainted Aunts*, *The Perfect Woman*, *The Anger of Aubergines*, and books on birds and trees for children. She teaches art to children with special needs and is a columnist with various newspapers.

Now That I'm Fifty!

stories of women who have scored a half-century

BULBUL SHARMA

women UNLIMITED
an associate of kali for women

Now That I'm Fifty!
was first published in English in 2011
by
Women Unlimited
(an associate of Kali for Women)
K-36, Hauz Khas Enclave
New Delhi 110016

ISBN: 81-88965-64-2

Cover design: Amruta Patil

Printed at Saurabh Printers Pvt. Ltd. A-15/16, Sector IV, Noida
and typeset at Tulika Print Communication Services,
35A/1, Shahpur Jat, New Delhi 110049

Contents

Now That I'm Fifty

THE day I turned fifty I began seeing things. At first it was just a few tiny specks and I thought I needed new spectacles. I was so proud of my ability to read without glasses till now. My late husband often said I would need them when I turned forty, but I could read quite well even when I was forty-nine and it always irritated him. He would offer me his specs every morning as we sat reading our newspapers, and I would give a polite little smile, shake my head and say "no". My poor kind husband, he has passed on, otherwise he would still be hoping for my eyesight to fail every morning.

Then a few weeks after I turned fifty, things began to appear. I saw them only for a second or two through the corner of my eyes. Tiny black arrows and dots at first, and then larger shapes. Gradually other things began to float into my vision, things I could recognize easily without turning my head. Open books would fall, mice, spiders and pigeons would flee past. Shirts, single socks and dupattas would flutter briefly then disappear when I turned my head. Once I even saw a pair of red high-heeled shoes, the kind bad women wore in films, totter past.

Then about six months later, one afternoon I was resting on the sofa after a light low fat, low salt lunch – my doctor had ordered me to lose two kilos or he would put me on blood pressure medication – I saw a woman scurry past. I rose from the sofa and shouted, "Who is that?" There was no reply. The door was locked and the servants had gone to their rooms behind the house. I called out again "Who ..." I wasn't afraid, not then.

Somehow, I had known from childhood that invisible people, animals and things hovered around me. I could not see them, but I heard them rustle or sigh very close to my skin. At night I could sometimes feel a soft touch on my face. My mother said I was blessed by the gods, but my sisters just thought I was soft in the head and refused to sleep in the same room as me.

It was only now, after I crossed fifty, that I saw something real. It was as if the gods were waiting for me to reach the right age and then bestow this gift on me. I think it is a gift.

I turned my head and saw her, a woman made of flesh and blood, though I am not sure she had either. This was the first time I had seen someone so clearly. I saw that she was wearing a grey sari, that the heels of her feet were cracked, though she didn't look poor or needy. She wasn't young yet she moved fast and moved out of my sight before I could call out to her.

I sat down again and thought for a while. If I told my sons about it they would smile uneasily, look worried and then think about taking me to a shrink. Not that I minded, it would be interesting to see what he had to say. I was sure my three sons – two of them dentists like their late father – would only take me to a male doctor. My youngest son who was a lawyer would declare me senile at once. In fact, he would be thrilled to hear about this condition of mine, treat it like a gift from the gods and totally take charge. "I always told Pitaji she is not capable of managing her affairs," he would say, rubbing his hands, and his rabbit-eyed wife would simper.

So I decided not to say anything to them yet. It might be better to see how things developed, as my dear late father used to say. He was a very successful lawyer but the real passion of his life was faith healing and nature cure. Whenever someone came to him for legal advice they went away clutching crystals or some root or bark in their hands. Later he stopped taking any cases and only saw people who wanted his faith healing not his legal skills. People came from faraway places with strange ailments. If he were alive today maybe he would tell me exactly what to do and take great joy in my condition. I would have been happy to oblige him.

I liked being told what to do. My father, then my husband, and now my sons always laid out my day for me. I nodded and pretended to go along. Though sometimes, soon after they told me what to do, they forgot and I could slip through the crevices and do what I wanted to. It was so easy. But most of the time I liked just going along the path laid out for me. It was too much effort to think on your own.

I am so shocked by how rude my daughters-in-law are to my sons, always back-chatting, making independent plans and refusing to obey instructions. Ma and Baba must be watching from heaven and their fingers must be itching to give the two girls a good talking-to.

Ma had a soft voice but when she wanted to she could raise it to cause real fear in people. She would stand tall and speak clearly, looking the person straight in the eye. Everyone always obeyed Ma without question. Even Baba who was so respected and feared in his office would bow his head before her. 'Do not be afraid to show your anger, girl, anger is what makes people do your bidding,' she would say to me. But somehow I could never really be angry with anyone for long. I began to feel lonely and afraid that they wouldn't love me anymore.

I often ask Ma what I should do or say and most of the time she replies, but I cannot really make out the sounds very clearly. But one thing is for sure – when I ask her to reprimand someone who has been rude or unkind to me, she always comes to my rescue. I had a great aunt who had an evil eye. The old relatives who saw her say she just had to look at you and your body would start trembling. You would break into a sweat and sometimes even get a rash on your skin. But Ma said that Great Aunt's evil eye often had a delayed reaction and would fall on people a bit late, very often after she had forgotten the feud and made up with the victim. They would be sitting amicably side by side sipping tea or shelling peas and then suddenly the evil eye would come into play without any warning. The lady would start trembling and her left eye would start twitching like mad. Great Aunt knew what was happening but she was helpless to do anything. She only had the evil eye and no antidote for it. Unfortunately, it was only women who became victims of her evil eye since Great Aunt spoke to no men except her husband, her brothers and her sons, and she would never cast her evil eye on *them*.

Not that I would cast an evil eye on my two daughters-in-law, ever. They were decent girls and their parents had sent huge dowries. They gave me saris and sweets on all appropriate occasions like Diwali, Holi, my birthday, the boys' birthdays, their wedding anniversaries and once for Christmas, too. But I refused to take that. "I am a good Hindu, and it might offend my dead parents who were also good Hindus, to accept any gift on Christmas." I didn't mind keeping the cake, though. It was rich with dry fruit and the fragrance was delicious. What harm was there in a cake? One ate cakes all the time. Cakes had no religious significance for us. It was like eating toast or biscuits with your morning tea. Jesus Christ would bless you if you ate cake. Anyway, our Hindu gods were so easygoing, they never really cared what you did as long as you prayed to them every day and offered them pure ghee sweets.

This afternoon I was watching TV as there is an afternoon serial I like a lot about a rich family and their feuds. It has deep social meaning and the women wear beautiful saris and jewellery. As soon as the serial began, I saw her again. This time she went past the door slowly as if she was tired and couldn't walk fast. But I couldn't see her face, I just caught a glimpse of her sari palla. It was red, with gold ambis – very much like the one I wore on my wedding. Everyone said they had never seen such a beautiful sari.

I do not go out much after my husband died, though my friends who are the same age as me travel abroad for holidays or to visit their children. Fortunately my sons live in our house. I should say my house because my late husband, a wise man, has left the house to me. In fact he left everything to me – houses, shops, the farm and the beach house.

I have made a Will but I haven't told the boys about it. Let them keep guessing, they will know when I die. Ma had my horoscope made by my uncle who became a sadhu after he retired from government service, and according to it I would live till sixty-four. So I still have fourteen years to go. I am in reasonably good health though my knees give me a lot of trouble and I cannot eat cauliflower any more at night because it gives me terrible wind.

I wish the woman would make up her mind and either stay or go. I'm irritated now with this silly hide-and-seek. Why doesn't she stay still, show her face to me? I was happier before she came when I saw only flying objects like teapots and shoes. You don't want teapots or shoes to sit beside you on the sofa and talk.

Last night I was greedy and had a bit of cauliflower and when I got up to look for some antacid, I saw the snake. It was lying curled up near the door. I stood still and watched it. For some reason I have never been afraid of snakes. Lizards terrified me but snakes, never. It was a thin black one with faint yellow dots and it raised its head to look at me. We stood for a while like this and then it slithered towards the window and went out. I took the antacid and got into bed. So many things coming and going made me feel quite tired. I closed my eyes and that is when Ma spoke to me, so clearly and loudly after a long time. "Baby," she said right above my left shoulder, "Baby, you must learn to stand straight. Otherwise you are going to get a hunch back. You're fifty now and must take care of yourself. This is the time the body starts going downhill."

"Ma," I said, turning around, and there she was lying on my bed eating an apple. She was always proud of her strong teeth. "All my own," she would say and flash a toothy smile at Pa whenever he took his dentures off.

"Ma… are you well? How is Baba?" I asked turning towards her, but I couldn't move.

"I am well, Baby, but you look terrible. What have you done to your hair? I always told you to wear your hair long and tie it neatly. Your face is too round and fat for short hair. You look like a fat schoolboy," she said, taking a bite from the apple. I thought ghosts didn't eat, they were supposed to pass through everything. But Ma lay there so solid, looking more real than she had when she was alive. Her skin was glowing like it always did, her hair – still black – was tied in a neat bun and she wore a garland of fresh mogra flowers. Things obviously didn't change much after you were dead. In fact it seems your skin improves. "Baby, I want to tell you that your Baba and I are not happy with the way the servants are behaving. You have to learn to be more strict with them. I have trained them well and now you are spoiling all that," she said fixing me with a stern look. I began to tremble. It was easier to face the snake than Ma.

"I try, Ma, but they don't listen. They're so rude sometimes," I said, looking at my feet. Though I was lying on the bed I felt I was standing before her in a short skirt and dirty shoes. "You do not try hard enough. Show some dignity. Look at you, roaming about all day in your dressing-gown with that stupid haircut."

I wanted to ask Ma about the woman with cracked heels whom I saw the other day, but she vanished just like that woman had. Everyone was in such a hurry these days, ghosts as well as real people. Every time I call my sons I hear a recorded voice asking me to leave a message after a beep. What messages can one leave? It's like speaking to someone without a body. It's like speaking to Ma. At least Ma shows herself like a real person, eating apples, coughing and belching.

Today I have decided to call the boys for dinner and tell them about the woman in the red sari. I will tell the cook to make saag meat, paneer and dahi bhalla. We will have gajar ka halva as dessert and some dark chocolate cake. It is an eggless one, the cake-shop lady said. The boys love this menu though their wives are always on a diet. Stick insects. Let's see what they say. Each one will try to give his opinion and the wives will sit staring into their empty plates. Maybe they count the silver cutlery, bowls and plates and calculate what their share will be when I am gone.

I will just listen. I don't have to agree to anything. I might see a doctor. It might be fun to talk to someone, someone not waiting for me to die. I will tell him about the flying objects, the slippers and the woman. But I won't tell him about my conversation with Ma. That is sacred and I must keep it hidden in my head till I die. After all, I still have fourteen years to go.

Afterlife

I DIED when I was fifty years old. I'm not exactly sure that I was fifty but when they were taking me to the funeral pyre, I heard people say that at least, by God's grace, she lived half her life. In our village most women, especially widows, live till they are a hundred, second wives till they are almost a hundred and ten. First wives with living husbands tend to die early, like me.

Of course, none of us can count so we just guess our ages according to which great event took place at the time of our birth. So we know which of us was born on the day when a great queen named Victoria who had ruled us for a hundred years, died. Those women always walked tall even though they were often short and fat. We know which of us was born during the great famine because those are the ones who cannot stop eating. However much rice you load on their plates, their bellies still moan like empty water-pots. Those of us who were born during the great earthquake which shook our entire mountain range, sank many villages, uprooted the old deodar trees like rotten teeth and brought a big portion of the mountain down, are the ones who always walk unsteadily like drunks and keep covering their heads with their hands as if waiting for the sky to fall on them.

Well, I was born during the great forest fire when the hillsides burnt for days and all the wild animals, jackals, bears, foxes and panthers ran into the village, their fur still burning. The birds had fled much earlier and every rooftop in the village had large flocks roosting on them, nibbling at all the stored corn and scattering burnt feathers all over the courtyards. But the snakes were burnt to death since they could not crawl away fast enough, and my mother said that for months they could smell their venom burning angrily, as if they were still trying to poison us even after they had died.

My mother gave birth to me the night a fox chased by a jackal came and hid in our barn. The jackal pounced on it, tearing bits of its tail off. The cows, frightened by this strange happening in their peaceful lives, made such a din mooing and groaning that my mother's childbirth screams were totally drowned.

She always felt cheated by all this drama taking place while she was crying and pushing me out, and complained to me often that there was no one to attend to her when I was coming into this world. Everyone was outside taking bets as to whether the jackal would catch the fox or be outwitted by the crafty animal. "They never fight, you know, the jackal and the fox, because they are both scavengers and each one follows the other, knowing there will be a kill close by. But the forest fire made them all go mad and they fought like cats and dogs in our cowshed." No one remembers who won the fight. Maybe only the poor cows did.

Fifty years.

They were good years God gave me. Of course there were minor irritations, like my neighbour's goats who always strayed into my fields and nibbled the tender wheat shoots, and the never-ending tooth troubles I had. Otherwise my health was very good. I had borne three healthy boys and was up and working in the fields exactly forty days later. I could have got up after two days but was not allowed to. "You are to stay away from the kitchen till your forty days are over," my mother-in-law said. Suited me fine. This was the only time we women got any rest.

Even when I was a young girl I was as strong as my brothers and could carry a heavier load of grass on my back. I was also quite tall for a girl, which annoyed my father and brothers so I had to bend my head very low whenever they came near me. I often got a stiff neck and had to stretch myself tall and touch the doorway when no one was looking. It helped to ease the pain a little.

I don't know how I just suddenly fell down and died. One minute I was cutting grass on the steep side of the hill – you know, where the goatherds build a make-shift summer home with straw and pine branches – and the next minute I was flying around looking down at my poor, helpless body. I had worn an old salwar kameez that morning since the day was fine and dry and I was going to be cutting grass all day. If I had known I was going to drop dead suddenly like this, like a sick hen, I would have worn a better suit. Not my best, I wouldn't like it to be burnt, but my second-best, the one my husband bought me from the Renuka fair last year.

But God doesn't give you a warning about your last breath. If only He did we could plan our lives much better, wear our best clothes, be bathed and ready for death. "Where are you going all dressed up, wearing your best slippers, new watch and new duppatta," people would ask and you would reply, "I am getting ready to die today." You could also settle scores with the people who had been mean to you just the day before you were going to be taken away because they couldn't do anything to you, could they? It would be too late for them to retaliate and later they couldn't speak evil of you because you would be dead. You could borrow money, say all kinds of rude words, eat forbidden foods you had been longing to and think of all the bad things you never thought of doing in case you were struck dead.

If I had known that I only had fifty years given to me, I would have done so much. I would have gone to the cinema in town, eaten ice-cream and been kinder to my poor husband even though he gave me so much grief. My husband was the only thing God had given me that I was unhappy with. Though my mother said this sorrow was all my fault and I had only myself to blame for my tears, I know it wasn't real grief that takes hold of you, eats you up like the death of a loved one. This unhappiness was light as air but always with me, a tiny nagging ache. My mother said it was something I had imagined like an animal figure in the clouds or the face in the full moon. "Your husband is a saint. You should wash his feet and drink the water every morning. You are lucky we found such a good man for you despite your being so tall."

I would rather have had a glass of strong, sweet tea than drink the water from my husband's washed feet which I am sure tasted foul. Though he did bathe once a week and change his clothes every ten days, his feet always looked as if they had been in a muddy ditch. That was strange because he was very fussy, my husband, and he washed his hands all the time even when he hadn't touched anything, wasting all the pots of water I had to carry home each day.

I was married to him when I was very little but went to live with him only when I was thirteen or fourteen. I know because my blood had started flowing that summer, and my mother told me not to touch the pickles. But I did, secretly at night, when the house was asleep and nothing happened either to me or to the pickles.

My husband's family came to fetch me the next day and I was quite happy to go with them. "Shameless girl, smiling like a monkey's backside. Try to look a little sad. You are leaving your father's house and will never ever return," said my grandmother, pinching my arm so that I would shed a few tears.

When I didn't she pulled my dupatta over my head, giving my ears a sharp twist at the same time. "That will stop you, you ill-mannered girl." I hid my smile behind the red dupatta. I was thrilled to be married, thrilled with the trunkful of new clothes and my new gold bangles.

My husband's village was right above ours. You could see it easily from our courtyard when the mist wasn't covering the hills, but it took two hours of walking to get there. I had to walk slowly this morning because of my new clothes, they were so heavy and stiff, unlike my old comfortable and soft salwar kameez. The sky was a clear blue above our heads but the forest looked angry and dark as we walked higher and higher, leaving my father's home behind. I didn't look back but I knew they must be watching us, afraid I would do some mischief and shame them.

There were sweet, ripe berries growing on shrubs along the way but I knew I couldn't rush out and pluck them. I was a bride now and brides weren't allowed to run. Not for a month at least. After that you took your red dupatta off, wore your old clothes and chased the cattle up and down the hill.

It was a long walk and the path was full of tiny stones that kept rolling off and making us slip. A flock of crows hopped alongside and my father-in-law tried to shoo them away by abusing them loudly. The crows abused him back, as they always do.

My husband, his kohl-rimmed eyes red, looked tired and kept whining that his new shoes were hurting his heels. "Take them off and carry them on your head, you spoilt sonofabitch," his father said. I almost laughed out loud and had to control myself. But I think my husband, who was so young then that he didn't even have a faint moustache, knew I was laughing and gave me a cold look. I didn't know then that I would have to live with that look for the rest of my life. The path became more and more narrow as we climbed higher and I had to step carefully, peering out from underneath the dupatta covering my face. My husband whined all the way and his father called him names like "delicate doll, nose-dripping sissy, cry-baby and mother's tail". The crows called out raucously above our heads and on this inauspicious note, my wedding party reached the village which was to be my home for the rest of my life.

Now you can travel up to our village by bus in fifteen minutes and my husband goes to town every second day, but in those days there were no buses. In fact I didn't travel in a bus till I was much older. When my first son was being born our village midwife couldn't manage to get him out. "Take her to the hospital or she will die," she shouted, shaking her fist at the men, trying to pull them away from their card game. My husband and his brothers threw me on a string cot and carried me all the way down the hill to the main road and when the bus arrived, they shoved me in the front seat like a bundle of old clothes. I kept screaming with pain as they argued with the bus driver about my fare. "She should go free, she is going to the hospital, you one-eyed owl!" Finally the driver agreed after my husband's brother threatened to break his jaw and also puncture the bus tyres. We all went free. My pains got less as I shook and rolled about in the bus, the rocking movement soothing my childbirth pangs, while my husband dealt out the cards behind me.

I called my first son Paploo, though his real name is Joginder. The other two were born safely at home and I named them Ramesh and Jitender but everyone called them Ramu and Chhotu. Their father just called each one of them "Oye". I think he could never remember their names.

My husband is not a bad man but somehow he never made

me happy. It was that cold, sullen look he had given me when we were children. He never looked at me any other way, it was as if he could never forgive me for laughing at him. I was a good wife to him, everyone said so, but he just wouldn't smile at me. For some reason it made me so unhappy that I cried myself to sleep almost every night when I was young. When I look down at the village now, I see him sitting outside in a patch of sunlight, playing cards. He is still very much alive despite his delicate health, though he does cough all the time.

Now he is making his second wife unhappy too. It's not that he beats us or gets drunk or anything, he just never notices you. You can shout at him, put too much chilli in his food, give him a damp kurta to wear, he will never remark on it, never look you in the eye with real anger, happiness or kindness. All he does is give you a cold look or stare blankly over your shoulders as if waiting for someone to arrive.

It was like being married to a wooden toy. He was indifferent to the children, though he bought them little gifts when he went to Shimla or to some fair in the neighbouring village, but he never played with them, never even scolded them or thrashed them like all the other fathers in our village.

He gave me enough money to buy rice, ghee and dal, bought me clothes too, every Diwali. I tried to be happy with all this. I told myself every morning when I brewed his tea, "He is a good husband. He doesn't beat you, he is not a drunk, he doesn't keep a woman in the other village. All he does is play cards all day and that is not a bad thing. So what if he doesn't smile? You can live without a smile or a kind look". My mother had told me all this and I tried to repeat what she had taught me everyday.

"A smiling husband? Who has ever heard of such a thing?" she said when she came to my house the other day, bringing me some freshly made ghee. She found me sitting by the window, my head tucked in my arms, the rice boiling over. "Wake up, girl. Clear all these cobwebs from your head. I don't know where you get these strange ideas from. Not from me, I'm sure. Your father was a good husband and beat me only if I put less salt in his food. That was the only thing that threw him into a rage. You could do whatever you wanted, but God help you if you put less salt. One day I was in a bold mood and I said to him, though softly , 'You can add some salt, can you not, if it is less?' And he gave me such a blow that I went reeling all the way across the room. Then he threw the thali at me but I managed to twist my head out of its way. He was a good man, your father, and the entire village respected him. Be happy girl, with the husband we got for you. A girl as tall as a tree, towering over all the men."

I often looked at other women in my village, they all seemed so content with their lot. Why was it that only I needed something more? Was there something wrong with me? Not only was I taller than any other woman I had ever seen but I knew my heart was different, too. My grandmother said it was all that snake venom burning in the air when I was born, but my mother said the cinema was to blame. As a young girl I had gone once with my brothers to the other end of the village where a man had brought a funny-looking machine inside a black box and set it up near the temple. As dusk fell, the box began to sing and everyone rushed to see what it was. The older people said it was the shaitan singing and stayed away but we children, all boys except for me, gathered near the box like bees, filled with curiosity to see what this man would do next. He unfolded a big white cloth and draped it on the wall, then before we knew what was happening, figures began to dance on the cloth. The women wore saris like town women and the men had shiny, curly hair like girls. They danced, sang and swore to love each other and smiled at each other even when the girl's evil father tried to lock her up in a cell. I thought it was magic and wanted to see it over and over again. When I came home I was thrashed by my mother and made to eat only dry roti for two days, for going to the cinema. I was the only girl from the village who had dared to go and no one ever let me forget it.

I never wanted my husband to have shiny, curly hair or to sing and dance, but I did want him to look at me and smile. My heart ached for that. But the years went by so quickly, my long black plait became grey but in my heart I still felt like a young girl. Even my heart grew old but it wouldn't calm down, it still ached gently like my knees, my feet and my back.

I am old now, I told myself. I have good sons, obedient daughters-in law, healthy grandchildren. At night before going to sleep I again told myself all this. But when I saw my husband's indifferent back turned to me, heard his loud grating snores, I often burst into tears. He never heard me, of course.

If only he had smiled at me once, that is all I wanted from him. A small gesture to say he knew I lived in the same house with him, that I was his wife and the mother of his children. Was it so difficult to do that?

Now I look down at the house from the clouds and remember how, when I was young, I tried so hard. Cooked his favourite food, made sure his clothes were washed and darned every week. His slippers I cleaned with oil so that mildew wouldn't grow on them. I managed the house well, too. The cattle were looked after by me since my husband never went near the cowshed. He would get a sneezing fit. "My son is very delicate, all this rough work doesn't suit him. He should have been a clerk in a government office. If only his late father had the good sense to send him to school," said my mother-in-law. I wonder if I will meet her now that I am dead, too. I hope not. She will accuse me of dying before my husband and making him spend all that bride money all over again. Actually she is irritated with me because I have escaped being a widow like her. I never have to wear white now and live in the back room of the house, eating only once a day. I never have to hide when a new bride comes to the village or not touch the food made for a pregnant woman. I was wearing a pink dupatta and red glass bangles till the day I died.

Gradually, bit by bit, I learnt to manage my heart. There are so many things in this life that give us joy and I learnt to look for them. A good crop, a cow giving birth to a healthy she-calf, rains on time to enable us to sow the next crop, and a mild winter when no child dies.

Then one morning I woke up and found I had forgotten all about my husband. I saw him sitting in the courtyard as usual, sipping tea, looking beyond me, and couldn't believe I had once cried for a kind word or a smile from him, torn my heart in shreds all these years. Of course, I cooked his meals, washed his clothes and mended his coat and caps but I didn't put my heart and soul into these chores. I too now looked at him as if he wasn't there. He continued to play cards behind the cowshed and I hardly noticed him. He could have been a shadow on the wall. I was now almost as content and happy as the other women. But then one day I fell down dead.

You should see my husband now, you wouldn't recognise him. He has become so thin, his hair is all grey and his cough is worse. But he still has his cold, sullen look. Another thing which really gave me a shock is that he cries all day and refuses to play cards. It seems he is grieving for me. I cannot believe it and look down often to read his face. Who was this man I lived with all my life? He never smiled at me once yet now he is shedding tears all day like a girl. His heart seems to be as torn with grief as mine was. He reminds me of the same boy walking up the hilly path with me, crying because his shoes hurt, but now he is crying for me.

His brothers forced him to marry again because they needed someone to take care of the house and the land, since our sons have moved away to work in town. This new wife who is much younger than him, tries so hard to please him. She makes tasty little tidbits and brings him hot tea but he only gives her the same cold look he used to give me. "Do not worry, girl. Learn to be happy without it," I shout to her but she cannot hear me. I see my poor husband sitting far away from our house on a rock looking up at the hill. I know he is staring at the very spot where I fell down and died. Now I feel so sorry for him. How did I know he would be so wretched after I went? He could have told me, the fool, while I lived, that I meant something to him. He could have smiled at me once. He had thirty-seven years to do it.

You know, I can count quite easily now, numbers no longer look like spiders to me. It's amazing how sharp my mind is, much sharper here in this cloud-filled world. But what use is it now that I am dead, and as my mother always said, "What use is learning for us women, just another headache." I see her every day now but she seems so young and unfamiliar to me. My father is nowhere around. I think they have separate compartments for men and women, like the toilets in the big hospital in town.

All day now I float above my village and learn things I had never known before. Secrets of other homes fly up to me like kites and I can hear husbands and wives whispering behind closed doors. I know which husband beats his wife and which wife gives her husband watered down rice-wine to drink. I know now that though all the women look content, their hearts are filled with longing which they try to tie tightly like a bundle of rags, throw in one dark corner of the house and forget. I also know that no man in our village has ever smiled at his wife or told her that he will go mad with grief when she dies.

We only get to know when it is too late – for both of us.

Salsa at Fifty

TWO years after my fiftieth birthday I decided to join salsa classes. I remember it clearly because that was the year my husband Ramesh left me and went to live in Goa with his secretary – a boy named Monty. I wasn't really keen to join, in fact I didn't even know that salsa was a kind of dance, I always thought it was a tomato salad type of thing you ate with funny triangle chips. Not the nice thin potato wafers which left your fingers greasy but a dry, slightly cardboard-tasting, papri kind of thing. I had seen people at parties dip these chips into the red sauce and eat them. The red juice always dripped onto their chins and clothes, so I avoided them. I hate getting my going-out saris stained – you always have to dryclean them.

Besides, this salsa thing was too spicy and I like plain snacks like cocktail samosas, or those round circles of bread with tiny dollops of some unknown black and red things you could eat without getting your fingers messy. At home one can eat anything anyhow and drop food all over the place, but I think when you go out you should nibble daintily, all nice and ladylike.

Anyway, my friends pushed me to join. "Sunita, you must go and do something positive," they all said after they settled down to have their second cups of tea. The first cup usually got cold because they were listening with open mouths to all that had happened. How Ramesh suddenly upped and went off with Monty, leaving his best suits and his Rolex gold watch behind. How Monty's wife appeared with a knife, looking for him. I wasn't sure whom she wanted to kill, Ramesh or Monty, maybe both, anyway she left after abusing them so loudly that all the neighbourhood servants came out to watch. The neighbours watched too, I'm sure, but from behind their curtains. I think she was Nepali, Monty's wife – she had sort of chinky eyes and was very slim, almost boyish. We had a Nepali ayah once who was very pretty and all Ramesh's friends always gave her a good tip though she hadn't really done anything for them. Poor Bhanu who sweated in the kitchen doing all the cooking, and Rana who served them so smartly running all over the place with trays of drinks, got nothing. But Ramesh never gave her anything, not even for Diwali. In fact, he found her very irritating and told me not to send her in with his morning tea when he sat in the garden. "Send Rana, instead," he said watching Rana as he hovered around us with a tray in his hands. I should have suspected something then but I was very innocent in these matters. I thought love could only happen between a man with a good job and a pretty, fair young woman. Nothing else was possible. Older woman and younger man, man and man, woman and woman were unheard of in my world. I still find it odd, this pairing of unlikely mates – a poor man marrying a rich woman or a very dark South Indian man marrying a fair Punjabi girl or the other way around, which is quite rare anyway. I mean, very few dark women find fair husbands unless they're very rich.

Ramesh and I were well matched, we both had wheatish complexions, our families were rich but not too rich, we both went to the same school and his mother played bridge with mine at the Gymkhana Club every Wednesday. His sister was married to my cousin. We could easily have been mistaken for brother and sister, except Ramesh is very handsome and I am quite ordinary looking; not plain, but not pretty either.

I thought we were happy. Ramesh was a good husband – a good man. He's still a good man. I don't know why I speak of him as if he is dead. Maybe the Ramesh I married is dead. I still don't know why he left me. He could have stayed here with Monty. We have such a huge house – five bedrooms with attached bathrooms, two sitting rooms, one formal and the one we use as a sort of den where the TV is and where all Ramesh's books – the not very serious, paperback kind – are kept.

But he did leave me.

I really didn't want to go out and do something positive. I was quite happy to sit at home and watch TV or read all day. I like historical romances best because you learn something and at the same time you're not asked to think too much about what you've learnt. Why read books that give you a headache and remind you of school? Murder mysteries, too, I love and my favourite is Agatha Christie. She has such a soothing way of writing about all these nice English people who are always polite and have tea in the library even after the butler has found a dead body in it. That could never happen in India. We create such a ruckus even when a dead rat is found in the drawing room. My mother-in-law would have had the whole house fumigated and the priest called for an eleven-day cleansing puja if ever a body was found in *our* library.

My son didn't want to talk about what his father had done. "Ma, it's awful. I can't deal with it, please don't ask me to. Makes me ill," he said when I told him. Now when I call him he just talks about movies or his ulcers. I like that, too. I wish my friends would forget about all this positive-thinking rubbish and just talk about gardening, movies and food.

It was my neighbour who first suggested these salsa classes, and I made the mistake of telling my friends about it. Pinky was quite plump – she must be about thirty, almost my daughter's age, though my daughter is very thin. "Aunty, come with me, it's a good, fun way to lose weight." I really did need to lose some weight, though now that Ramesh had gone I was wondering if there was any need to. Who would notice if I was fat or thin? My daughter might comment but it would be something like, "Oh, Ma, just flow with the energy."

She was planning to become a Buddhist but hadn't quite made up her mind yet. It would be tough for her to become a vegetarian because she loves her meat curry and egg bhujia.

Ramesh had sent her to Oxford hoping she would become something important when she came back, a lawyer or banker. But Sheena decided to join an NGO instead. She gave away all the expensive designer clothes she had bought when she went to Paris. Now she only wore cotton kurtas and baggy salwars. Their colours ran when the maid put them in the washing machine with our clothes, so now they had to be washed separately by hand. Sheena doesn't live with me. She has a barsati in a new colony which I have never been to, but when I mentioned it to my friends they made a funny face so it couldn't be very nice. She comes home often to have her clothes washed and to pick up her mail. She always tells Bhanu to cook meat curry for her. It's not easy to become a vegetarian at this age, I tell her. Your body will get a shock and your hair will turn grey.

She too said I should join some classes. "Dad leaving you has been a great trauma and you need to get rid of all your negative energy. But not salsa, that's awful. Hope Babloo didn't ask you to, it's just the kind of cheap thing he would do. Why don't you join yoga classes or do meditation instead? It will slowly wipe out your loss."

I haven't felt any loss as yet but I did try yoga. Then, during one of the asanas when you have to fold your arm behind your back, I tugged too hard and my arm got stuck. They had to take me to a doctor who gave me an injection to free my arm. Meditation, too, I tried when Ramesh took me to a nature camp in Rishikesh. (He hadn't met Monty then.) They told us to sit quietly and let the thoughts flow through our heads. But after a few minutes I started feeling so dizzy and this funny feeling came and settled right in the middle of my forehead. It sat there for a long time like a big invisible boil. I still get it sometimes when I shut my eyes in a crowded place. Meditation isn't easy for people like me who find it difficult to sit cross-legged on the floor. My thoughts don't seem to flow either.

They hover above my head and then swoop down on me like a kite. Ramesh was quite good though, and sat still for a long time, letting his thoughts flow, a strange smile on his face as if he was planning something naughty. Well he was, wasn't he?

Pinky said I should wear loose clothes for salsa because you have to jump about and stretch quite a lot.

"Is it safe for me?" I asked

"Yes, yes, lots of aunties come there. Boski lets you do it at your own pace."

I was a bit nervous on the first day, I'm not very happy about meeting new people. When I was to meet my older son Babloo's future in-laws, I got these flutters in my heart although they are very nice, polite people with a good business in woollen garments in Ludhiana. Their daughter went to a convent school and she is a good daughter-in-law to me. Ramesh sent our son Babloo to the US to study because he was afraid they would turn out a peculiar NGO-type like Sheena if he went to England. He was right as usual. Babloo is a vice-president in a multinational company and has to wear smart clothes even on Sundays when he plays golf with his boss. Unfortunately, he doesn't get along with Sheena though there's just a year's gap between them. I had my babies one after the other and now that I think back, just as well that I did. Ramesh hadn't planned Monty then.

Every time I try to have the family over for lunch it turns out to be a very unpleasant occasion. Babloo and his wife come on time looking very smart, carrying their cell phones, and Sheena always turns up late with a bag of dirty clothes. She invariably says something rude to my daughter-in-law about her nail polish or tight jeans and then Babloo leaves without having the pudding.

The children don't mention Ramesh's name anymore and it's very awkward for me. It's not as if he's dead or anything. I still talk to him on the phone and he sends me packets of very good quality cashew nuts with people coming from Goa. They're usually young boyfriends of Monty's and they always stay for lunch. They tell me Ramesh often talks about me and Bhanu's cooking.

I would like to go and visit them some time. My friends say Goa is lovely in winter and many foreigners have built beautiful houses on the beach. But Ramesh hasn't invited me and I don't like to be pushy. Maybe I will lose some weight with these salsa classes and then I can surprise them by turning up in Goa in tight jeans. Ramesh liked tight jeans.

The music was too loud and the hall was filled with the smell of women's sweat and perfume. Boski came up and gave me a hug. I wasn't sure I liked that. How can you hug someone you've never met before? I only ever hugged my children, that too only if they were crying or ill. Older people, when someone died in the family. Ramesh and I never hugged each other – it would look so funny, as if we were brother and sister instead of husband and wife. Already we looked alike. (Though Ramesh used to hug Monty a lot when he came over to our house before they went away to live in Goa. They would laugh, box each other on the chest and then hug. And they often held hands at the dining table. I used to think it was so friendly and sweet, then look what happened. I don't trust hugging anymore.)

Boski took my hand and said, "Come on, sweetie, don't be shy. Let it all flow. Loose. Let your body l-o-o-s-e. Come … come … hey ho, up you go … " she said, and gave me a gentle push. I almost fell down. Why do people always ask you to flow? Do they know how dangerous it is?

"One-two-three … One-two-three, bend … one-two-three, bend and twist … bend and twist… Warm up nice and sweet now. Stretch … yes, yes. Let it go, let it flow! Once again, my beauties," she shouted, opening her mouth wide. I noticed she had a gold tooth.

"Where is she from?" I asked Pinky on our way home. My whole body was aching but in a nice way. I felt as if I was floating in a warm sea.

"Oh, I don't know. Maybe she's Russian. Could be Polish. Somewhere abroad but she can speak Hindi, so better be careful," Pinky replied, smiling at me. Her plump, baby cheeks were flushed with sweat and she looked very pretty.

"The other day one of the women, you know the one who wears a red scarf around her head, well she said something in Hindi, I think it was … *Bolti bahut hai, sali mem,*" and Boski replied at once, "*Hanh, mai to bahut bolti hoon aur aap bahut moti hain.*" We both laughed and the driver looked at us in the rear-view mirror and smiled. It was so nice to sit with someone who's not your husband or child or a relative and laugh like this, like schoolgirls.

I have no complaints about my husband. Ramesh has been

very generous to me. He pays the servants and gives me pocket money every month, much more than I need.

"It is his duty ...," say my friends, "but don't give him a divorce ever."

Ramesh hasn't asked for one.

He can't marry Monty – his dead father, an upright army man, would turn in his grave. His poor mother, still alive and quite fit for an eighty-five year old, cannot really understand what has happened. "Why does he spend so much time in that Goa place? I'm told it is full of dirty hippies," she said to me the other day. But Sheena says she knows because she heard her tell Bela masi, "*Hai Ram*, Ramesh lesbian *ho gaya hai.*"

Sheena thinks it's a big joke but Babloo and his wife are very ashamed. They worry constantly about what people will think, what the servants will say.

"Why couldn't he run off with a woman? Surely there were female secretaries in his office. Why shame us like this by going off with a boy, for God's sake. What will I tell my son when he grows up?" Babloo said to me the other day. It was very unusual for him to talk so freely, with so much emotion, but I didn't know what to say to comfort him. When children are young you know exactly what to do to make them happy. It's so easy to love them and comfort them, but when they grow up it becomes so difficult to find the right words. Babloo and Sheena get offended so easily that I just kept quiet. I think they blame me for Ramesh's flight to Goa. Sometimes I blame myself, too.

"Stretch like a cat! Arch your back and look right into my eyes ... Okay, breathe slowly ... you are floating in air. One

... two ... three ... one-two-three, my lovely. You're doing so well, clever girl!" Boski's hand was on my back. She pulled my arms and then let go gently. A faint musky scent came from her as if she had been in some forest full of wet flowers. She looked at me and smiled. Suddenly I felt dizzy but not in that meditation, boil-in-the-forehead kind of way. I felt dizzy in a happy, excited way. I used to feel like that when I was a child and my father swung me too high on the swing. I could feel my heart thump with the fear of falling and then flood with joy, knowing my father would catch me when I came down.

"Stretch your arms, sweetie ... now move with me. One-two-three ... one ... two ... and three and four! Throw your head back like this ... once more. You can do it!"

I tried but my arms suddenly became stiff as I remembered the yoga incident, but Boski jabbed a finger in my waist and laughed. "Come on, Miss Roly Poly ... try and try !"

Each day my body got lighter. I hadn't lost any weight but I could move faster now. I felt as if someone had chipped bits of my body off and made me hollow so that I could jump up and down and twirl around, as frisky as a puppy. I put on the music, not too loud in case it woke my mother-in-law, and tried to do the steps at home but it was no fun. I needed to see all those other women swirling around me, needed to hear their loud voices, raucous laughter, smell their sweat. Boski kept us moving faster and faster. Sometimes it was salsa, then rock and roll, then some Bollywood kind of hip-shaking dance. As I shook my flabby body to the strange unfamiliar music, I began to shed layers of memories, of hurt, of blame. I jumped in and out of my body like a snake, feeling younger and yet much older. I saw my parents looking at me with horror, my in-laws in disbelief and then finally, Ramesh's face loomed out of the dimly lit room, staring at me in admiration. He had never ever blamed me for anything.

The music blared and some of us sang along loudly and discordantly. No one cared. We all looked at each other and smiled like children playing truant. Oh! We aunties and the slender young girls, how we laughed as we crashed into each other, twisting our bodies into funny poses, raising our heads like vain peacocks, and I knew I could never be a dancer.

But then I could never be so many things in this life. I tried so hard but failed to be a good wife, a good hostess and a good bridge player. I cannot sing or play the sitar. I cannot cook dal like my mother-in-law, I couldn't even learn how to drive or use the computer.

Now half a century has passed and I am quite happy to just let things be. I'm happy that Ramesh is happy. I have some years left to hug my comfortable self – ten, twenty, maybe even thirty, who knows? My lifeline on my palm is crooked so it could mean anything.

I know that I will always dance the salsa clumsily, I will always talk to my children awkwardly and cannot be a wife to my husband except in name.

But now it seems all right. I don't know why, but it does.

Strangers in the Park

THE man was staring at her from behind the palm tree. Sudha began walking faster though she was already on her third round and feeling quite breathless. The trees had begun to change colour as the weak winter sun dipped suddenly without warning. There were still plenty of people walking in Lodi Gardens, a few old men were sitting on benches and lovers lurked in the shadows of neem trees. There was nothing to be afraid of. Sudha didn't turn her head but she saw through the corner of her eyes that the man was still staring at her. He was walking along the jogging track but his head was turned towards her as if he was waiting for some response. He was younger than her and looked like a foreigner or an Indian who had lived abroad for a very long time. He had that pale, clear skin untouched by heat, dust and spicy food. It was a healthy, salad eater's complexion. She took another quick surreptitious glance and noticed his hand was in plaster. That made her feel a bit less anxious. An injured man was a safe man.

Suddenly the man stopped and touched the leaves of a shrub

near the path with his unbroken hand. "It is a morpankhi," she heard herself say, loudly and clearly, to her horror.

The man smiled and nodded."Oh. Thank you for telling me. And that one over there with large floppy leaves?" he asked pointing to a kanak champa. She quickly named the tree and started walking again at a brisk pace, her eyes looking straight ahead as if she was a sailor on a ship searching desperately for land. The man jumped across a bed of pansies with graceful ease and began walking with her.

Sudha didn't know what to say. It was her fault. She shouldn't have spoken to him in the first place. All her life she had been warned never to speak to strange men however well-dressed or fair-skinned they may be, and now she had gone and done it at the ripe old age of fifty-three.

"What is that tree with fern-like leaves?" he asked, leaning towards her as if they were old friends going for a stroll in Lodi Gardens on a winter morning.

"A gulmohur," she said curtly, not looking at him.

"And the one next to it?" he asked politely.

"A banyan," she said. What kind of man didn't know a banyan tree? Even foreigners knew what a banyan looked like.

"No, not that one, I know what a banyan looks like. The one with a dark bark behind that huge peepal."

"An allstonia," she said. She mustn't talk to this man any more. He was trying to be too friendly, smiling too much. Sudha forced herself to walk faster. Her heart was thumping in her chest and she hoped she wouldn't get her palpitations. She had just started these walks after her doctor told her to do some moderate exercise. This was becoming more than moderate, bordering on strenuous, in fact, which the doctor had told her to avoid. She might faint. Sudha pressed her finger-tips like her yoga teacher had told her to do in case she felt faint.

They had almost reached the old bridge. What if any of the regular walkers saw her with this man, she thought nervously, looking around. A flock of parakeets flew across and landed on the ruined wall, announcing their arrival in screeching voices.

*

"Is that a cassia fistula?" he asked. His accent had a trace of some European language, either French or Italian, mixed with Punjabi. Sudha relaxed. A man who knew his cassias couldn't be a crazy serial killer, besides his hand was broken. If anyone saw them she could always say he was a cousin. But then she would have to ask his name. "I am Ranjit. Ranjit Singh," he said and put his left hand out awkwardly. Sudha nodded, feeling quite light-headed with relief. It was alright. It was a respectable name. She knew several Ranjits and they were all quite harmless. Now if his name had been Bobby or Vicky or something racy like that, she would be wary and never respond to him.

As they walked, a bit slower now, she pointed out all the trees and shrubs to him. She was quite pleased that she knew all the names, and he seemed interested even in the wild flowers that grew like truants in the flower-beds. They discussed the merits of some of the winter annuals and the trouble of growing various varieties. This was the first time in her life she had talked about seedlings, grafting and manure to someone besides her old mali and it made her feel strangely alert and happy. It was as if she had a mind of her own and this stranger knew it. Another group of parakeets flew across, screeching louder than usual, as if they were warning her about talking to strangers. Ahead of them the maulsree and jamun trees created a shady avenue, and suddenly it seemed to her that it was darker today than other days. She mustn't imagine things. Soon this man would go his way and she hers.

They walked through the dimly lit green tunnel and then suddenly emerged into bright daylight. A stray dog chased a crow, barking in a half-hearted way, and three elderly ladies walked by slowly, all talking loudly at the same time. "Forget about respect or obedience these days, no daughter-in-law has heard of it. You should be happy if they offer you a glass of water," said one of them in an angry voice.

Sudha tried not to look at Ranjit but she knew he too was smiling. One heard such odd snatches of conversation in Lodi Gardens and Sudha amused herself by imagining how the conversation would continue as the walkers went ahead. She always walked alone since no one in her family was very keen on coming here. "I like to do all my walking in shopping malls. You will be amazed at how much exercise you get looking at shops," her sister-in-law said. Her daughter-in-law thought it was too crowded and her mother-in-law, the old aunts and uncle could barely walk. Her kitty club ladies did walk here but she didn't want to join their intense gossiping sessions.

"I'm really grateful to you for telling me their names. The flowers are the same as there, but the trees confuse me. You see, I have been living abroad – in France – for thirty years now, though I was born in India, in Karnal. I knew some of these trees quite well as a schoolboy."

Then he must be around forty, Sudha thought, looking at him for the first time. He was very tall and thin, with thick, curly hair going grey, and stooping shoulders. He looked like a professor. A professor of botany, maybe, but his English was tinged with a faint government school accent. It sounded very odd because he also pronounced many words with a French accent.

"I am in import and export, mostly garments," he said. Sudha felt her heart lurch with disappointment. Her father used to say "import-export is another term for smuggling". But this man with light brown eyes and slender hands – at least the one she could see – couldn't be a smuggler. Anyway there was nothing to smuggle from or to India anymore. Drugs? No, never. No drug dealer would be able to tell a cassia fistula from cassia albezzia. And why should she care what he did? She was never going to see him again.

"Would you like to have a cup of coffee with me?" he asked hesitantly.

"No... no... I have to go now. My driver is waiting," she said quickly, looking around her as if old Babu Ram was lurking under a tree.

"Well. It was very nice to meet you and thank you again for pointing out all the trees to me. Tomorrow I shall repeat them to myself, one by one," he said, laughing as he waved goodbye.

*

Tomorrow. That means he is here for a few days. Sudha quickly got into the car and told the driver to take her to the

Club. She didn't want to go home in this agitated state. She was still quite breathless and she could feel her face was flushed. She had done something so bold and so reckless that her family would be shocked if they ever found out. Had she told him her name? No, she hadn't done that, thank God. He wouldn't be able to find out where she lived and follow her there. Tell everyone in the family that they had met and walked together in Lodi Gardens. Had discussed winter annuals, seedlings and the merits of green manure.

*

The sun was much stronger today and the gardens were bathed in a bright light which danced on the lawns and skipped over the grey stones. Sudha had finished her first round and now as she approached the bridge, she saw him. Should she slow down or walk faster and overtake him? Either way she was sure she would meet him. Then while she lingered, pretending to fix her shoe, she saw him take a left turn and then suddenly turn around. They met face to face. Sudha didn't know what to say so she pointed at the Krishna ficus.

"Oh, hello. What is that?" he asked coming towards her.

Sudha picked up a leaf from the ground and held it in her palm. The curved leaf had a small, neatly shaped pocket and a big black ant crawled out looking quite surprised. Sudha burst out laughing.

"It's a Krishna ficus. Bet you didn't know that," she said giving him the leaf along with the ant.

"Err… Will the ant bite…" he said taking the leaf hesitantly in his left hand.

"Yes, it bites very hard and will not let go of you even when its head is snapped off," she said, trying to look serious.

Ranjit placed the leaf back on the ground and both watched as the ant crawled out and disappeared into the grass.

"This tree is called Krishna ficus because of the shape of its leaves. They say baby Krishna ate butter with it and later wore it on his head as an ornament," said Sudha as they started walking together. Today she didn't feel nervous at all, it was as if they had walked together like this every evening, amongst noisy parakeets, brisk joggers and shuffling old men.

She learnt that his father had a big textile shop in Panipat and his mother was a schoolteacher in Karnal, where he was born. He had left India at eighteen for France, first working as a steward on Air France. Then he began importing cotton shirts from India. He was one of the first to do so and did extremely well. He began selling to big stores in the US and lived in California for a few years, where he met his wife. But he came back to live in France after his wife had died six years earlier of cancer. Now he just travelled all over the world, looking at gardens and monuments. He had two sons who lived in the US. One was a professor at Yale and the other a ski instructor. They were not married though they both had live-in girlfriends. He had broken his wrist in Jaipur when he slipped on a banana skin. He told her all this very quickly and with amusing details, as if he was miming someone else's life, as if he was a character in a comic strip.

"Can you imagine someone actually slipping and falling on a banana skin? I thought only Charlie Chaplin did that, except he never bumped into an angry cow," he said and showed her how he had skidded on the street. Sudha suddenly had a fit of giggles. A couple passing by smiled at them.

How silly of her to laugh like a girl. She must behave herself or else he would get the wrong idea. It wasn't proper at her age to laugh loudly in a public place like this. She was trying to compose her face into its usual dignified lines when she saw three ladies from her kitty club walking towards them. "I must walk faster," she said under her breath and lurched forward. Ranjit, taken aback, began walking faster too. "No… you stay back. Please, stay back," she whispered urgently, not looking at him.

"Hello, Sudha,"said the women, one by one, as they slowed down to pass her, checking out Ranjit from head to toe without breaking step.

"My cousin! From France," she shouted at their retreating backs which had disapproval writ large on them. She knew what they would say as soon as they turned the corner.

Sudha felt her feet drag on the path and the trees bent low to cast a shadow on her. She had known that someone would see them and it was foolish of her to walk so close to him, giggling like a schoolgirl. Had the women heard her giggling?

"Now that you have declared me a cousin will you have dinner with me tonight?" asked Ranjit, smiling at her.

"Who… me…?" Sudha uttered, her heart suddenly giving a lurch.

"Yes, your husband too."

"My husband died ten years ago."

"Oh. Sorry to hear that... But if you are free ... it would be lovely..."

Sudha hung her head. She knew this would happen. He was trying to pick her up now. He thought she was a woman of easy virtue, a woman who talked to strange men in parks, who giggled and laughed with reckless abandon. How could he think such a thing! This was a most respectable park where senior government officials and their wives walked, where old ladies came for yoga. She had seen a Supreme Court judge here the other day, walking his dog. How dare he? Maybe it was her fault. She had encouraged him by showing off, telling him all the names of trees and shrubs. She had got carried away by his friendly charm.

Ranjit looked at her.

"Hope you don't mind me asking you out to dinner? It's just that I thought it would be nice to learn a bit more about the trees of Delhi. You're the first person I have met who knows so much. Would you prefer lunch?" he ventured.

She should just tell him to buy a book. There was a very good one out recently on the trees of Delhi by Pradip Krishen. She should do that. But what harm was there in having lunch with him? She had never gone out for lunch with anyone except her late husband, that too along with his entire family. They used to go to Kwality's every Sunday and they always ordered the same thing. Lunch with a strange man! What would the kitty club ladies say? Maybe she could take Shama with her, that should be all right. No one could point a finger at her then.

"Yes… lunch would be fine, but I will bring a friend, if you don't mind?"

"Great. Would you suggest a good place?"

"Machaan – at the Taj."

That was safe, so well lit and full of family parties. Her kitty club went there but if she bumped into one of them, Shama would be with her and she could pass him off as Shama's cousin from France.

As soon as her car moved out of the gate Sudha began to panic. What had she done? She was going for lunch with a man she had just met yesterday in the park. What would her family say? What would Babu Ram say when she told him to drop her at the Taj hotel? She never went anywhere alone except to walk in Lodi Gardens. She must call Shama at once.

*

Sudha looked around the dining table as she spread butter on a stack of toasts. Her late husband's uncle dozed in his usual chair, occasionally slapping his face gently as if to chase away an invisible fly. He was ninety-six and could barely recognise any one of them now. His two younger sisters, both in their mid-eighties, sat next to him, bickering in soft tones like they did every morning about something that had happened sixty years ago. This morning they were quarrelling about a film they had seen during the second world war. Her mother-in-law watched them with a sour expression on her face, keeping a wary eye out for any misdoings by the servants. She smiled with joy when she saw the servant boy, a new recruit, put the quarter plate on the wrong side and pounced on him. "Fool, how many times have I told you … are you deaf … not this side, not this side. I keep telling you, you idiot," she shouted, twisting around in her chair. The old man woke up, slapped his cheek and then shut his eyes again. The aunts stared at the boy for a moment and then resumed arguing. "She didn't elope, she was kidnapped … by a dacoit … I remember the dress she wore… " Sudha sighed and moved the plate to its correct place. Then she began handing out the buttered toasts to them one by one.

"Can you pick up Maya from school, Ma? My driver has to take the car for servicing," her son asked as she passed him a toast.

"I'm going out for lunch … to the Taj … to Machaan … with Shama aunty," she said quickly and her voice sounded too loud even to her. The words seemed to bounce on the old bone china plates given by her mother for her wedding, thirty years ago, hit the mirror and then crash on the table where the family sat. The senile uncle, the bickering aunts, the servant-spying mother-in-law, her beloved son – they all knew she was lying.

"That's nice, I can drop you," said her son, smiling at her above the newspaper.

"No… no, I am going with Shama. She will pick me up."

"Ok. Then Babu Ram can fetch Maya from school."

There. She was stuck without a car and driver now. This was the first lie she had ever told the family and God had punished her at once by taking Babu Ram away. Her old faithful driver who had come with her as part of her dowry thirty years ago. The aunts had suddenly fallen silent and were looking at her strangely, and even the old uncle seemed more alert than he had been in the last ten years. Sudha peeled an orange and passed it to her mother-in-law but she refused, and taking her ever-watchful, hawk eyes off the servant boy, she fixed them on Sudha.

The old lady could always read her mind and now, on this winter morning with the sunlight sparkling outside on her beautiful lawn, her double pansies in their finest bloom, she could see that Sudha was going to become a fallen woman. This is the reason why in olden days all widows had to shave their heads and wear white. The elders did that because they knew that a heart still fluttered in a widow's body and it could betray her at any moment. A kind word or a quick glance from a strange man could set her on fire. A widow was a plant that hadn't died completely even though its branches had dried up. A few drops of water could revive her and, God forbid, make her bloom.

"It's only lunch, why are you making such a fuss? Just because your stupid family lives in the dark ages?" said Shama, her voice lazy and indifferent. She yawned, then asked, "Who is this man, anyway? Someone we know?"

"No, we don't know him. He lives in France somewhere."

"A Frenchie? Wow!"

"No. Indian – Ranjit Singh…"

"Oh. I know several Ranjit Singhs – Bunny, Sibbi and Tony. Is he from the Kapurthala clan, the French branch?"

"No. He is from Karnal."

There was a sudden silence at the other end.

"I don't know anyone from Karnal," said Shama, her voice alert and suspicious now.

"His father has a cloth shop – in the wholesale bazaar," Sudha said quickly. Might as well get all the information over with.

"What!? Bloody hell! What is going on? Well, I'm glad you asked me to come along. Don't say or do anything till I get there," ordered Shama and put the phone down quickly.

The lunch was a disaster. Shama was quiet at first, watching Ranjit through narrow eyes, and then when he began talking about trees and shrubs she lost interest and began playing with the cutlery on the table. Ranjit tried to include her in the conversation but she ignored him and only talked to Sudha, looking at her watch every few minutes. Then she took her cell phone out and began sending text messages, looking up at Sudha from time to time. Finally Ranjit asked for the bill.

He took out a gold card and handed it to the waiter. Shama looked at his wallet with frank curiosity but when he tried to talk to her, she turned her back to him and started telling Sudha about some school friend's birthday party in great detail. Sudha ignored her and tried to talk to Ranjit, but he seemed very amused by what Shama was saying and watched her with a polite smile on his face.

As soon as they got into the car Shama began screaming at her. "What are you thinking of? Thank God you had the good sense to take me along! I only hope none of our friends saw us at Maachan lunching with this … Ranjit. The man is a lower middle class upstart who has somehow got to France and made money. Lisping away like that as if he is Omar Sharif! You can tell at once he is from some stupid municipal school. Sudha, you must be mad, even talking to someone like him!

When you said Ranjit Singh I thought he was Timmy or Bunny Singh's cousin. He's a nobody and comes from nowhere. Karnal! For God's sake. Who on earth lives in Karnal?" she shouted, taking her sunglasses off. Sudha could see her eyes blazing with anger.

"Well, lots of people do. I have seen huge crowds crossing the road whenever we pass by on our way to Kasauli. Even the Shatabdi stops there. It has a lake, people say, and you can go boating," replied Sudha. "Anyway, you had no business being so rude to him. He is my friend."

"Sudha, you just met him yesterday. And you know very well what I'm saying. Millions of people live all over India but we don't have lunch with them, do we? We meet people who are like us. Whose parents knew our parents and who were at school with us or our brothers. I can't believe you had the guts to go out with this odd person who cannot even pronounce 'breakfast' correctly. I won't be surprised if he puts mustard oil in his hair and spits paan on the road."

Sudha didn't say anything, just looked out of the window. A group of women were working on the pavement, carrying bricks on their heads. They chatted and laughed as they lifted the bricks, helping each other while their children played in the mud near their feet. A baby slept in a makeshift sari hammock in the shade of a jamun tree. Suddenly Sudha felt she needed fresh air, needed to get out of the car which was filled with Shama's perfume. "Stop, I want to get out here. Please … I want to go for a walk. I must get out here," she said to the driver and Shama shook her head. "Do as you wish. You need to get your head examined. Hope this man is not here! God, I thought Lodi Gardens was a safe place. Sudha, please, please watch out," she shouted as Sudha jumped out onto the pavement, slamming the car door shut.

Sudha stood at the gate. The late afternoon sun was quite bright and the path had a mosaic pattern forming on it which kept dancing. She felt a bit dizzy as she walked quickly towards the octagon tomb. Two young girls walked by very quickly and she heard one of them say, "He could either be a homosexual or a womaniser, but not both."

The palm trees stood like sentries guarding the old monument which had been cleaned up recently. Sudha missed the old black walls scarred with graffiti but she knew this was better for the monument. She knew what was better for her, too. She must not become involved with this stranger. Her children, her in-laws, her parents and her friends would be devastated if she did anything so bizarre. She must walk the straight line like all the other widows or single women her age and behave with proper decorum. She must play rummy at the Club, go to the Chinmaya Mission with her mother-in-law, lunch with her friends and play with her grandchildren. She was a middle-aged lady and soon she would be old like the aunts. She too would sit around the dining table and bicker gently about what had happened half a century ago. That was as good as it was going to get for her. She remembered the lines from a film of that name and smiled.

Anyway, why was she getting so worked up, it was not as if Ranjit was asking her to elope with him to France. All she had done was have one lunch with him and gone for a few walks. They had never even talked about anything else but trees and plants. Soon he would leave India and she would never see him again. Her life would settle down once more, a bit breathless and shaken, but otherwise as normal, safe and dull as ever.

"Now which Lodi is buried here?"

Sudha's heart jumped and she turned around quickly. She didn't expect him to be here at this time, but when she saw him she knew she had been hoping all along that he would be.

"I have been reading about the Lodis," he said, smiling down at her. "They were real warrior-kings – quite ruthless, but I love their architecture, so rugged and yet majestic."

"Sorry. About lunch ... my friend. She was a bit ... she was not..." Sudha mumbled, not looking at him.

"Listen, forget about it. Good friends are always very protective. Come on, let me show off my new-found knowledge about the Lodi dynasty to you," he said, touching her elbow gently. They walked slowly around the tomb, Ranjit pointing out various features she had never noticed before. The gardens were quiet now with just a few malis dozing in the warm sunlight. Soon the regular walkers would arrive and her gang of friends would see her walking with Ranjit again. She didn't care. She looked up and smiled at him and he, startled, smiled back. They walked quietly and then Ranjit picked up a flower from the ground and gave it to her. Its petals were faded and crushed but when she held it to her face, the heady fragrance of the dead champa sank into her skin.

*

Sudha pushed the plate of barfi away and looked at her watch. There were still four hours to kill before she could go for her walk. Maybe she would go to Khan Market and look for a book on Delhi to give to Ranjit as a farewell present. She would write something simple and friendly in it. A sudden wave of sadness swept over her as she saw herself walking alone in Lodi Gardens, looking at the monuments and recalling what Ranjit had told her about each one.

"You're not eating at all nowadays, what is the matter? Are you in love or what?" her sister-in-law asked, laughing as she reached for another barfi. The women sat in the garden after lunch with their knitting. In half an hour they would go into the house for their siesta. The mali watched them from underneath the bougainvillea canopy, willing them to get up and go indoors so that he could settle down for his nap under the trees.

Sudha looked at her watch again. Only fifteen minutes had passed. She picked up her knitting and began to unravel what she had made last night. "Mummy, can you give me the white baby wool please," said her daughter-in-law who was very fair and plump. She wore pink and white all the time and often looked like a fluffy ball of wool as she sat placidly on the chair, smiling vaguely. Sudha was fond of her though she had never been able to talk to her or find out what made her happy or sad or angry. She was a polite, well brought up girl, soft spoken and gentle-eyed and her son seemed very content with her.

I was like her too when I was young, thought Sudha. Pretty, placid and plump, an ideal daughter-in-law. And now I am a middle-aged woman, thin and discontented, talking to strange men in parks, going out for lunch with a man whose family is in the wholesale cloth business in Panipat, a man totally unknown to us.

Sudha looked at her watch, still only half an hour had gone by. She wondered what Ranjit was doing. Did he know anyone in Delhi besides his business people? What did he do in the evenings? Sit alone in his hotel room? Read books on trees?

It was two weeks later that the storm broke. Ranjit, two days before he was to leave for France, asked her to go with him. He didn't ask her to marry him, just go for a holiday to Europe with him. He wanted to show her the gardens of Versailles. "Then we will go and see Monet's garden in Giverny and drive around that region of France, stay in small inns."

She stared at him, her eyes round with fear. What was he saying? How could she go for a holiday with a man? A man who wasn't her husband or father or brother. Was he asking her to live in the same room with him? How could he do such a shameless thing? Sudha wanted to cry with rage. This was all her fault. She had talked to a strange man and all her life her mother had told her what happened to women who talked to strange men. Now it was happening to her. He was asking her to become his mistress.

"We can get cheap rooms if we book right away. You could ask your friend Shama to come along, too, if you like. I have a large house in the country," he said.

So he was not interested in her. Why should he be? She was fifty-three years old, not some pretty young girl with a sexy figure. He must be surrounded by them in France. Why should he want someone old and boring like her? Someone with grey hair and wrinkles around their eyes.

"I don't know, I must ask my family. I haven't been abroad for a long time," she said, trying to sound casual and indifferent.

"Well, I'll come and meet them. I would like to in any case, if it's all right with you."

The aunts fixed four pairs of unblinking eyes on him while the old uncle greeted him like a long-lost friend, slapping his cheek over and over again. Her sister-in-law gaped at him and her mother-in-law just narrowed her eyes and sniffed the air like a fox terrier. Her son was polite but cold. Her daughter-in-law giggled nervously when he asked her what she did.

"In our family the women do nothing except instruct the servants about what to make for breakfast, lunch, evening tea and dinner," said Sudha laughing. Ranjit smiled as the family closed rank and stared at them with fear and suspicion, as if they were aliens who had landed in their drawing room from another planet.

Slowly and determinedly Ranjit drew them out, one by one. Like a general who knew what his enemies were thinking he began by making inroads to the most hostile ones. He started with her son, asking him about the shares market and then discussing various financial trends. Then he turned to her mother-in-law and asked how she kept such a beautiful home, servants being what they were these days. Then the old aunts, chatting about old movie songs, even singing one quite well. At last he turned to the old uncle and talked to him in a soft, soothing voice about the weather. To her daughter-in-law and her sister-in-law, he displayed his Cartier watch and matching handkerchief. By the time the evening settled into darkness and the garden filled with soft shadows, her family had taken him into their fold and chatted away happily, as if he were an old friend.

As she watched him bring the faded old drawing room to life, Sudha made up her mind. She would go to France with him. She would go alone. They would see all the famous gardens, eat in wonderful restaurants and see all the great museums and ancient buildings. She owed herself this. God had sent her this stranger on a bright winter morning and she wouldn't let this last chance of her lifetime go. She would travel with Ranjit, be his friend, companion or whatever. Then she would come back and spend the rest of her life around the dining table. Slowly, she would grow old and bicker like the aunts, probably become senile like the old uncle and slap her cheeks happily all day. Suddenly she could see clearly into the future and knew this was as good as it would get – but she would steal thirty days for herself. She would wrap those golden days around her like a warm shawl and inhale its fragrance for the rest of her life.

Thirty days of joy. After fifty-three years of giving, it wasn't too much to ask for, was it?

Birthday Surprise

MADHU folded the shirt and placed it gently on the pile of clothes lying on the bed. It had come neatly folded from the hotel laundry but she didn't like the way it was done, the collar looking as if it was trying to escape from the rest of the shirt. She sighed as she took the tissue paper out and brought the sleeves together in one swift movement. Madhu loved folding clothes, but not as much as she loved arranging flowers or cutting fruit into complicated shapes. Everyone in the family, not just hers but Jeevan's too, remarked on her expertise at each and every household task. She could manage to have a dinner for twenty people at one hour's notice; she could coax her old cook never to go on leave; she could detect even the smallest fudging of household accounts by just sniffing the air in the kitchen, and her garden won the first prize every year.

Even her mother-in-law who was an acknowledged empress of housewifely skills reluctantly agreed that "our Madhu is a good housewife," but added, "She's not much to look at though, but you can't ask for everything in the daughter-in-law department these days."

Madhu smiled to herself. She knew she wasn't a pretty face but her husband Jeevan called her his perfect mate. She knew more about him than he did himself and could complete most of his sentences for him. She knew what he liked or disliked, what he wanted to eat or to wear, where to go, whom to meet and whom to ignore. She knew every little detail of his business and he always asked her for her advice before doing anything. Yes, she was his 'ardhangini', his better half, and she didn't know what he would do without her.

Today was her fiftieth birthday and Jeevan had brought her to this beautiful place called Pattaya so that they could celebrate, just the two of them, away from the family. "A honeymoon once more, my dear," he had said, winking at her at the breakfast table. His mother saw it and made a face. His sisters narrowed their eyes with envy. Madhu hid her smile and quietly spread sugar-free jam on her husband's toast.

Actually it had been her idea to come away for her big birthday. At home she would have had to call the entire family and plan everything. She would have liked to have just her own two daughters and their husbands over, but that would never do. Jeevan's four sisters and their children, his mother, his unmarried aunt who lived with her, his various nephews would have to be invited or they would feel very hurt. Then her own three sisters and their half a dozen children could not be left out either.

So last week she had quietly, very gently, begun to talk about going away for a few days. Every night just before he went to sleep she would press Jeevan's head, rub tiger balm on his forehead and whisper, "You need a break, a change will do you good. You work too hard, you need some rest." And sure enough the thought she had planted in his head grew quickly like a tiny well-watered seedling. One day it blossomed and he announced, "I have been thinking of going away for a few days. What do you think?" Madhu expressed her delight and said how clever he was to read her mind, "I would love it!"

Next morning she casually placed some brochures near his cup of lemon tea, and now here they were in this wonderful hotel in Thailand in a beach town called Pattaya. There had been a few tense moments when her mother-in-law said she wanted to come along too and bring her unmarried sister for company, but Madhu nipped the matter in the bud by saying that she had checked and there were no more rooms available at their hotel.

She loved this place. She had been abroad only twice before, to London, where it had rained all the time. The English were not friendly and she didn't blame them – there were so many shabby-looking Indians roaming the streets. It was embarrassing. She was sure the English thought she was an airport-cleaner type too, so she always made sure she wore her best silk saris and biggest diamonds when she went out. Jeevan travelled to London every summer for a month to look at all the new watches but she didn't go with him. Besides, her mother-in-law wanted to go along each time so Madhu always refused when Jeevan asked her to. Poor chap. He always looked so crestfallen, he couldn't manage without her even for a day.

This beach town in Thailand was so much better. It was just four hours from home, the shopping they said was very good, the food had lots of chillies and the people were nice and friendly, smiling all the time. Of course, Jeevan had a bad habit of tipping everyone who did even the smallest chore for them, especially the girls. "Poor things, so pretty," he always said.

*

Madhu went to the window and drew the curtains. She looked down at the busy street where flower-vendors lined up every evening and hawkers brought all kinds of strange fruits to sell. She wanted to go and buy some but wasn't sure whether it was safe to go out alone. And she didn't know the roads here. At home the driver knew exactly where to go without being told.

As she watched, a motorcycle rode up, scattering the crowds, and came to a noisy halt in front of a house with a red door. A young girl dressed in baggy black pants and a tight red t-shirt jumped off and ran to the door. She didn't wave or look back at the man but when she got to the door, she looked up and saw Madhu. She smiled, making a funny face like a little girl and Madhu, surprised, smiled back and waved at her hesitantly.

Their room overlooked this busy lane behind the hotel, always choked with traffic and people who walked in and out of tiny shops and cafes. Many of them were foreign men but they all seemed to have Thai wives. "It's strange that so many Thai women marry foreigners. I wonder what their children look like?" Madhu said to Jeevan but he just laughed loudly. Jeevan wasn't very happy with their room because he wanted a sea view but Madhu convinced him this was better and cheaper. "When will you look at the sea from the window?

We will walk there if you want," she had said, taking the key from the hotel desk.

They hadn't yet gone to the beach or done any shopping though this was their second day here. Yesterday Jeevan had met an old friend from school and they had gone to look at some watch shops. "All fakes. You should see how well they copy the designs, Madhu." Jeevan looked very excited and happy to be here, totally unlike his usual sleepy self. His skin had an unusual glow as if it had been polished with oil and his eyes darted about excitedly. This holiday away from the family was doing him a world of good. Today he had gone out with this friend again to see a watch factory. When she asked him where this school friend lived, Jeevan looked startled.

"Why do you ask? Here. He lives here. I told you yesterday. He's in the watch business too, but very worried about this fake stuff and wants my advice. How can I refuse him? School friend and all. Tomorrow I'll ditch him. Your birthday, after all," he said, and went out of the room quickly before she could tell him her birthday was today.

Jeevan's family owned the oldest watch shop in Delhi, and in the days of the Raj all the British people bought watches from his grandfather. They had framed many of the letters and bills they received from their English customers, even the ones who complained that the watches they bought didn't work properly, and hung them all over the shop.

Madhu saw some more girls coming around the corner of the lane and going into the house with the red door. The girl in the red t-shirt came out with a bucket and mop and began cleaning the steps outside. After a few minutes she stopped, leaned back and looked up. Madhu smiled and waved to her. The girl laughed and asked her to come down. She pointed to a bucket of flowers near the door. Just then another motorcycle rode up and two girls got off. It must be a girl's hostel. But why would they come here in the morning?

Madhu looked at her watch. It was almost noon. Jeevan was taking a long time at this watch shop. They were to go shopping to some flower market. At night he had planned a river-cruise dinner for her though she was not sure she wanted to have dinner on a boat. What if the water they cooked in wasn't clean?

There was also a surprise gift for her. She knew what it was, of course, but pretended not to. He was like a child, always wanting to please, to surprise her. It got quite tedious pretending to be surprised and overjoyed when she knew all along what his next move would be.

Where *was* he? She would wait another fifteen minutes and then call him. She turned away from the window and saw to her surprise that he hadn't taken his phone. How irritating, she said to herself and lay down on the bed to wait. Was it her imagination or was he behaving a bit oddly here? Had he forgotten her birthday? How could he? Yesterday they had talked about it and planned where they would have lunch today. Why had he gone with this stupid school friend? Let him do his own worrying about fake watches. She would have to be a little stern with Jeevan when he came back, she couldn't allow this kind of behaviour at this late stage in their marriage.

It had taken her years to get Jeevan to behave exactly the way she wanted.

They had been married thirty years now – next week was their thirtieth wedding anniversary. She couldn't remember what her wedding day had been like thirty years ago when she was only twenty. Was she a great organiser then too, like now? Had she planned her own wedding? Her mother never said anything except that she was a clever student and they were sure she would become a lawyer or a doctor. But then they found her a good husband and got her married quickly. "Better than being a lawyer or a doctor," her mother said because people respected you more if you were married. It was true. As Mrs Jeevan Rai she got so much respect wherever she went. Shopkeepers gave her unlimited credit, bank managers got up when she came into the bank, and during family weddings the bride and groom always touched her feet first – after their parents' of course.

But arranging flowers, cutting fruit perfectly, keeping a sparkling clean house where guests could drop in any time and find freshly starched hand towels in the bathrooms, being better than all the other women at cooking, baking, knitting, making pickles, killing cockroaches and mice did not bring her as much joy now as it used to.

In a few hours she would be fifty. For some reason, for the last few weeks she had been thinking about her life. She had never thought like this before and it felt strange, as if she was turning into another person. These new thoughts were disturbing and she tried hard to block them but they came streaming in. Earlier all she thought about was who liked what for lunch, whether to order dal or just a gravy dish, which servant was about to give her trouble, had the dhobi brought the clothes in, was her cake going to win the prize at the Club again? Nice, comfortable thoughts that kept her days organised and running on a safe track and lulled her to sleep at night.

But now at odd moments, like when she was bathing or just about to fall asleep, these new unfamiliar thoughts came rushing in. Like insects they buzzed in her ears. Who was she? What had she done with her life? What had she really done for herself? What did she want to do for herself?

Her husband, her daughters, her mother-in-law were all taken care of by her. She arranged their lives, they couldn't manage without her. It gave her a great sense of satisfaction to see them depend on her, look to her for every little thing. But who was Madhu? Who was *she*?

Fifty years had gone by in a flash and now the time left to her should be her time. But did she want it to be her time? Did she need it like the others needed her? She didn't know what she would do if she didn't have the house to run and all these people to look after.

How silly she was to think like this. It made her dizzy and gave her a headache. Made her afraid too, as if the ground beneath her feet was trembling. She wouldn't allow such thoughts into her head. She was Madhu who was good at everything, her cakes were the lightest and her chrysanthemums had won a gold medal this year. She was Jeevan's beloved wife and he would be back soon. She should wash her face, comb her hair, put on lipstick and wear her sari.

It was quite hot outside because the girls were wearing tiny shorts like schoolboys, so she would wear her new pink chiffon with the gold ambis. Her old pearl necklace would do. Jeevan had bought her a heavy gold necklace with an ugly diamond cluster pendant – yet another tedious surprise. It was sitting silently in his suitcase, glittering away secretly, waiting to surprise her in the evening. She had seen it in the morning when he was in the bathroom and didn't like the design at all, but she would clap her hands in delight and say it was lovely, just the kind of necklace she had always wanted. It was important to keep her charges happy at all times.

Madhu looked at the pink sari hanging in the cupboard, its embroidered palla moving gently in the breeze from the air conditioner, and stretched out her hand. A slow wave of weariness swept over her and she continued to lie on the bed. The traffic noise, muffled by the glass windows, hissed and moaned outside and soon she was fast asleep.

It was dark when she woke up. She got out of bed quickly and looked at her watch. Nine o'clock! She had slept for eight hours. A sudden fear rose in her heart as she looked around the room. Why was Jeeven not back? Why had she slept so long? She walked to the phone and began looking for the Reception number. There was no answer from the desk. She sat down on the bed once more. Her head felt heavy and she wanted to lie down again but she rose and went to the cupboard. She pulled out a sari, not the pink chiffon but a plain travelling one, and picking up her handbag, she went out.

The lobby was crowded with a group of German tourists. They were all men, most of them old with shocking white hair and pale, grey faces. One of them bowed to her and smiled. Madhu frowned and went to the desk. A pretty Thai girl looked up and smiled at her. She had no idea what to ask. How strange it would look if she asked this girl with long eyelashes and pink rosebud lips where her husband was. How would she know? Madhu asked her if she knew where the nearest watch shop was but the girl smiled and said, "No. Not know watch shop. No have here watch shop, lady."

Madhu nodded and moved away. The old German, or maybe he was Swedish or Finnish or some other white variety of man, stared at her from behind the pillar. He was making strange gestures with his fingers now and shaking his head. Madhu looked away. The street outside, now brightly lit with fairy lights, was teeming with people. She could hear loud music blaring and shrill laughter even though she was inside the glass door of the hotel. For the first time in her life Madhu felt helpless and lost.

Suddenly she was out of her depth. She who was such an efficient woman, coping with everything that came her way effortlessly, now wanted to sit down and cry. She must control herself. Jeevan was fine and would be back soon. He was just looking at watches and must have forgotten the time. She forced herself to smile at her own joke. He knew it was her birthday and he knew she would worry. He had been gone for almost nine hours, but would be back any minute. He was her husband. Depended on her, needed her. She tried to calm herself but suddenly a wave of fear overcame her. What would she do if he didn't return? Who would she call? This would never happen at home – everyone knew where everyone was at any given moment. But this was a foreign country, she couldn't just pick up the phone and talk to the police commissioner, who was a personal friend at home.

She saw herself become smaller and smaller till she was a tiny mouse in a cage, going round and round on a toy wheel. She only knew how to function in her own safe world surrounded by a circle of admiring relatives, docile servants and an obedient husband. Here she didn't know what to do, whom to call, bark orders to. The Embassy! Should she call the Embassy if he didn't come back by midnight? He had to. It was her birthday and he was her husband.

But what if he had had an accident and was lying in some hospital unable to speak to the Thai people, unable to tell them who he was? She must find him, he was lost without her.

Madhu was sick with worry now. She wanted to go back to her room but the grinning man was standing near the lift so she sat down on a sofa near the door and looked out. The house with the red door looked different now. A big blue neon sign flashed on and off, painting the walls and changing the colour of the door from red to mauve and purple. People, mostly men, crowded near the entrance.

Then suddenly she saw the girl in the red t-shirt come out. How strange that the only familiar face was this girl's whom she had only seen twice before. Madhu got up and tried to catch her attention. The girl looked at her and waved, pointing to a bunch of flowers in her hand. She would go out and talk to her, buy some flowers. It would help to pass the time, clear her head till Jeevan came back. There was nothing to fear. All she had to do was cross the road.

Just as she was about to go out of the glass door the girl from the reception desk came up to her. "Call for you. It's your husband."

Madhu almost ran to the desk and snatched the phone from her. It had a strong perfume of jasmine. "Madhu, Madhu," she heard Jeevan say. His voice sound strange as if he had a bad throat. "Jeevan, where are you? I have been waiting all day," she said, her worry turning to anger as soon as she heard his voice. "Listen, I am in a real mess. Can't talk. Please bring money, a thousand dollars, to the Honey Rose Beer Bar behind the hotel. A man will meet you. Bring cash. It is in my black briefcase. The necklace – bring that too. Don't talk to anyone. Please Madhu, please come quickly," and he broke off.

Madhu stood frozen by the desk, her hand clutching the phone. The jasmine fragrance circled her and then settled on the gleaming reception desk. The pretty Thai girl smiled and nodded her head. The German man disappeared into the lift, still grinning and waving to her.

Madhu felt the warm, damp air on her face as she walked out of the hotel. The street was jammed with cars, auto rickshaws and crowds of people all dressed in flowery shirts. She crossed the street blindly, tagging along with some women who were carrying bunches of red and yellow flowers. Cars honked at them and the women giggled, waving the flowers. They looked like the giant lilies that grew in her garden at home but Madhu couldn't remember their name. She clutched the bag with the cash under her arm, feeling its soft leather grow damp in the heat.

She found the Honey Rose Beer Bar quite easily because it had a huge red sign gleaming in the dark. The outside porch was crowded with foreign tourists who were all wearing only shorts and garlands. Some of them smiled and called out to her. She waited outside, feeling naked and exposed in her sari and long-sleeved blouse. Then a girl came up to her, took her by the hand and led her to a door on the side of the building where a few hawkers were frying fish. She said something to them and they all laughed, staring at Madhu. The girl rang a bell with a smiling Buddha's face on it. Madhu frowned, her fear melting into anger. It was not right to press Lord Buddha's face like this, so disrespectful and inauspicious, too. The door opened at once. It was dark inside but she could hear people talking and laughing loudly. A high-pitched voice sang somewhere far inside. As her eyes got accustomed to the darkness, she could see the girls. They were running around everywhere and they were naked, except for a glittering band around their waists. Madhu opened her eyes wide in horror and then, suddenly, felt a strange desire to laugh loudly. Her hands twitched as she covered her mouth and tried to stop herself from laughing. Must not get hysterical, she thought over and over again, as she watched the girls flit from table to table like fireflies.

So this is what this place was. A house for bad women. Jeevan, her beloved Jeevan, had come to this place to look for girls. They had been married thirty years and she never thought her husband was a man who would come to a place like this. Now when more than half her life was over, she had to make this ugly discovery. He had punished her with this on her very birthday, as if this were a present she would have to look at. A real surprise at last.

A girl came up to her and asked her something. Madhu couldn't hear her and took a step back nervously. "Drink, you want drink, lady?" Madhu shook her head. The girl shrugged her shoulders rudely and walked off. Madhu saw that she wasn't naked but wore a transparent body-suit like babies wear at night to keep their legs warm. Except hers was so tight it showed her thin ribcage and her tiny breasts. She couldn't have been more than fifteen or sixteen.

Madhu watched her move among the tables offering drinks, laughing when the men pinched her bottom or jabbed her breasts with their fingers. She didn't know whether she should ask for someone or just wait. Jeevan had told her she would be met. Why did he have to pay this man so much money? Their entire holiday cash? The answer came to her through the dark room. He had bought these girls … She tried not to think of what was happening to Jeevan. As she looked for him in the gloomy, foul-smelling room a sudden rage filled her, edging out all her fear and pity. "Serves him right, the old fool. To behave like this at his age," she said loudly to herself and immediately felt much calmer.

She moved behind a pillar and looked around the room. There was a stage at one end where some girls were dancing in a sleepy, languid way as if they were not really there but in some faraway dream land. She saw to her surprise that there was a group of Indian men laughing and clapping at them. She was sure they were Indian because she could hear them call out to each other in raucous voices, saying terrible things about the girls dancing on the stage. Madhu wanted to go up and slap them but she stood rooted to the spot. What had Jeevan got himself into? She should never have allowed him to go out alone with his stupid school friend. At home she always made sure they only met people she approved of, people with proper breeding, good backgrounds and education. People whose fathers and grandfathers knew Jeevan's father and grandfather.

Just then a tall girl wearing a flowing robe walked up to her but when she came close, Madhu saw it was not a girl but a man. He came and stood still right next to her, his face gleaming in the shimmering light. "Good evening, madam. Hope you are well?" he said bowing to her. He was neither Thai nor Indian nor European. His face was yellow, but he had large, long-lashed eyes like a girl and he wore red lipstick. Madhu began to feel afraid. "You brought me something, I think. Your husband said you will bring me a nice gift," the man said, smiling at her.

"Where is my husband?" she asked, surprised to hear how firm her voice sounded. She would cope, everything would be all right. She knew she would cope. "Your husband is with us. He loves to party, you know, but he had a little fall down the stairs and hurt his legs. We took care of him," said the man, holding his hands out to her. She saw that his nails were painted red. "May I have my gift, please. Look, you can see your husband, he's there, sitting on the chair, enjoying our club. So young at heart he is, your old man," he laughed. Madhu looked towards the corner where the man's finger pointed. Jeevan was sitting on a chair, his head thrown back. Both legs were bandaged. A girl was sitting on his lap. She looked very young and very bored.

The next few days passed in a haze. Madhu got Jeevan admitted to a hospital. Both his legs were fractured and his face was badly cut. He could see only with one eye as the other was black and swollen. He refused to talk, just stared out of the window when she visited him, tears rolling down his one good eye. "Tell me what happened. Where is your school friend? How did you fall down the stairs? Did someone beat you up?" she asked him over and over again but he just stared at her, his eyes round and stupefied.

Madhu sat in the hotel room alone and watched the lane all day. All kinds of terrible thoughts came and settled on her though she tried hard to brush them aside. She saw the girl in the red t-shirt every morning and suddenly one day, decided to go and talk to her. She didn't know why but she felt she needed to hear her voice. The girl was surprised to see her. "Do you speak English?" Madhu asked. The girl looked up, then nodded. "A little bit. Thoda, thoda," she said and laughed. She wasn't pretty like the other Thai girls, her face was flat like a peasant's and she had strong arms and rough hands. Her name was Soumai and she lived in a village an hour away from Pattaya.

Madhu sat with her every afternoon while Jeevan slept a drugged sleep in his hospital room. Other girls came out and sat with them. Gradually she got to know about all their lives. Soumai was not a bar-girl as the others were called. She just cleaned the place and did all the washing and ironing for the others. Every morning their fathers and brothers and husbands dropped them off to the house with the red door and picked them up the following afternoon since the girls worked on alternate days.

"We get very tired dancing, dancing all the time. Men want happy, smiling girls not sleepy, tired girls," one of them said. She had a young son at home. He went to a good school and came first in his class every year. The girls sat around in the veranda outside the bar in t-shirts and crumpled shorts, looking like schoolgirls. In fact they *were* schoolgirls who didn't go to school anymore. "Why you wear this big red dot, why you wear so many gold bangles, so many diamonds. Not safe here," they said to her as they tried her stick-on bindis. "You are very pretty, lady, white men really go for a dark beauty like you," they said and made her wear plastic flowers in her hair. It was the first time anyone had called her pretty.

Madhu was surprised at how easily they talked to her, a strange woman from a foreign land, and how comfortable she felt with them. They told her about their families, their childhood illnesses. One of them, a frail girl with large doe eyes showed her her appendix scar. "One German man paid for operation. German men good, spend a lot of money on us. Pay for husband, brother, too. Buy motorcycles, watches."

Soumai was teased relentlessly by the other girls for some reason, so one day Madhu asked why. "She is in love with Indian boy. Handsome, fair Indian boy from Bombay," explained a girl with a sweet, crooked smile whose name was Mayhee or some such which Madhu couldn't pronounce.

Soumai looked at her shyly, then took a wallet out carefully from her belt and showed her a tiny passport-size photograph. A boy with a big nose and tiny eyes smiled back at her. "His name Samir. He come and marry me one day soon," she said and collapsed laughing. The other girls fell on her and they struggled together like playful puppies, giggling and laughing loudly.

Madhu was amazed at how cheerful they were despite their ugly lives. They sold themselves every night to anybody who was willing to pay the going price. They were somebody's daughter, wife, even mother, but it didn't matter. They were nothing to anyone. She stayed awake at night thinking about them. What if she had had a life like that? What if God had sent her to live here where she had no home, no family; where no one needed her except a bunch of paying clients?

How different her life was, or was it really? Had she also sold herself to Jeevan and his family? Had she no identity of her own? But she had so much respect, so much money in the bank and a huge house to live in. Everyone admired her skills and needed her. That was enough. It should be enough. But who was she? Who was Madhu? Who was Mayhee, the girl with a sweet, crooked smile? Who was Soumai with the rough hands?

After fifteen days Jeevan was discharged from the hospital. Madhu had earlier phoned home, asked for money and said they were staying a bit longer. No one questioned her, they were used to her taking all the decisions in any case. They came back to the hotel to pack their things. Jeevan looked thin and his eyes still had a stupefied look. He seemed to have aged in the last twenty days. "You forgot my birthday, my dear, for the first time in thirty years," Madhu said as she packed their bags. "Did I? Sorry. I know I did. Sorry. Sorry for everything. Never thought they would…" he choked and began sobbing. Madhu left the packing and went up to him. "Let us forget whatever happened. You are all right now and we are going home today. You will be home soon."

Madhu patted him as if he was a child who had cut his knee and come running to her. She wanted to say, "Hope you've learnt your lesson, you stupid, stupid man," but she thought that could wait till later when Jeevan was a bit stronger.

She would take care of him as she had always done, but she knew their life would never be the same again. The shadow of this ugly holiday would always hover above them. She would never be the same again herself. Her entire mind had been pulled out and then put back again in a strange, new way. Who she would be now she had no idea, but she wouldn't be the same. She had glimpsed another life just when she was climbing uncertainly up the ladder of her own life. Suddenly there were so many other worlds spinning around her, so different from her well-ordered one, and one of them had collided with her and left a mark that would stay forever.

"Come, let us go," she said trying to keep the sharpness out of her voice as she helped Jeevan get up from the chair. She took one look outside the window before they left but there was no one sitting on the steps. It was getting dark and the girls, the fireflies, had begun their dance.

Should She or Shouldn't She?

NIMMI picked up the silver salt-cellar and passed it to her husband. He looked at it, took off his glasses and looked at it again. "Needs polishing," he said and put it back on the dining table. They continued to eat in silence. The toast, warm and crisp, just the way Mohan liked it, crunched loudly as he chewed. No one said anything because Mohan did not like chatter at the breakfast table. Till he had finished his fried eggs, sunny side up, toast and marmalade, very bitter, and second cup of coffee, he wanted no conversation around him at all.

They all waited – Nimmi, his mother and the dog. She was always the first one he spoke to. "Walkies, sweetheart?" he said, his green eyes twinkling. And then he turned to his mother and said. "Slept all right, Ma?" Then it was Nimmi's turn. She had been married to him for thirty years, but even now a wave of panic rose in her stomach when he turned his bulging green eyes on her. "Make sure the silver is polished before it all turns totally black," he said, and nodded to Jano who was standing near the door with his coat, cap and walking stick.

Mohan got up from the table and came around to help his mother as she struggled to get out of her chair. Nimmi sat watching them quietly. She never helped because neither mother nor son liked it. It was a daily ritual which made both of them feel better about each other.

She picked up the tarnished salt cellar, placed it next to its pair, the pepper pot, and wondered why that was less tarnished. Maybe pepper had some hidden qualities that prevented moisture from scarring it. Maybe it was just luck, like some women ageing so beautifully while others looked haggard at forty.

Nimmi looked out of the window at the garden beyond.

Today was her fiftieth birthday.

She had been born half a century ago in a small town called Koti in the foothills, two hours from Simla. Her father was a wealthy landowner and her mother a full-time housewife, like most other women of her generation, though there was a cousin in the family who went abroad and became a lawyer. But no one ever spoke about her and if they did, they always began with a sigh and said, "Poor thing, never got married."

*

Her mother was quite surprised when Nimmi was born after four sons, and never recovered from the shock. Every time she saw her she would exclaim. "Where has this girl come from? So dark and tall. Who will marry her?" Then she would turn to her husband and say, "Are you listening? You better give her a huge dowry. They say the darker the girl, the heavier the gold she has to bring. And then she is tall, too. So we might have to throw in a house and car as well."

Everyone was amazed when she married Mohan, the only son of Khemchand Khanna, the richest family in the entire Simla region. They owned apple orchards, ice factories, several shops and a cinema hall called Paradise Talkies on the Upper Mall.

"Maybe the boy is an alcoholic," said some unkind aunts as they watched the barat march in.

Her father had given her a grand wedding, though a much smaller dowry since she was marrying into such a rich family. His boys could well use the money he saved. But Mohan's mother never forgave her father for it.

"She has brought nothing, not even a new car for Mohan or a new pearl necklace for me," she would say to visiting relatives, fingering her double row of natural pearls.

Nimmi had been married now for thirty years, and for thirty years she had sat at this dining table and watched her mother-in-law butter her husband's toast and cut it into small bite-size pieces. The only change had been in the colour of the bread which was brown instead of white, ever since Mohan's cholesterol was found to be on the high side.

It seemed like nothing had happened to her in the last fifty years, she had just floated from one house to another. From whenever she could remember she had heard her father and brother talk about politics, land disputes and guns, and now she heard Mohan say the same things in a louder voice. Her only child, a son, lived abroad with his family and she only saw her grandchildren on the computer, waving to her once a week on something called Skype.

If she dropped dead right now on this polished dining table, surrounded by tarnished salt-cellars, no one would notice for weeks. Her mother-in-law would blame her sudden death on the lack of dowry and Mohan would be angry at the mess she had made. "Why couldn't she die on a hospital bed like everyone else, instead of scratching the dining table like this?" he would remark, and the poor servants would have to polish everything all over again.

Mohan liked everything to be exactly the way he wanted; an inch extra, a milligram heavier would not do. The furniture in the vast house had been arranged according to his directions and if anyone moved a table or chair by mistake, he would fly into a rage.

"This chair remains here!" he would shout, thumping his walking stick on the floor. Fortunately the servants had all been in the family for years and knew exactly what went where and how.

The toast, brown bread baked at home, was put in the toaster the minute Mohan's footsteps were heard on the corridor leading to the dining room and the toast popped out as soon as he sat down. His fruit was cut by Nimmi but placed on his plate by his mother. He had very light tea with just two drops of milk and Nimmi's hand sometimes shook when she had to pour the milk. But most of the time he did it himself with a sad shake of his head. "Nimmi, darling, when I say two drops of milk I mean two drops, not two and a half. Please try and pay attention to what I say."

Mohan selected the saris, the shoes and the shawls she wore, but luckily she could choose her own undergarments. He told her how to tie her hair in a bun or a plait, and since he hated short hair, she had to keep her hair long even though it wasn't as thick and black as it used to be. She oiled it at night hoping this would make it grow thicker, but only when Mohan went out of town because he hated to see oil in her hair.

Mohan also directed his mother's life and told her which medicine to take even if her doctor had prescribed something else. Since she only wore white saris he couldn't choose her clothes but he did tell her which slippers to wear. The maid had to bring them all out and he would point to one or the other with his walking stick.

Before he left the house for his office in Simla, he told both of them when to go for a walk and where, which book to read and what to order for lunch. He had already told Jano about what to cook for dinner and how. "Tell Ram to fry it very lightly. Make sure he doesn't overdo it, otherwise the meat gets tough," he said as Jano helped him into his jacket and handed him a clean handkerchief. As his car rolled down the driveway, he shouted at the mali, ordering him to trim the shrubs by exactly one inch, not more.

What he did for the rest of the day Nimmi never knew but he must have enjoyed ordering the workers in his shops and factory. She sometimes wondered whether he went into the cinema hall and told people which film to see. Since there was only one evening show they would have to obey him.

*

Nimmi got up from the dining table and went into the garden. The sunlight fell on the lawn where not a single weed dared to grow. A tiny blue butterfly flew past her and settled on the rose bush, scattering a few old petals. Was a butterfly too heavy for the rose, she wondered, as she went closer to inspect its beautiful blue wings. As soon as she bent down, a pied flycatcher swooped down and caught the butterfly. Its blue wings fluttered for a moment and then disappeared into the bird's beak. "What a short and happy life," said Nimmi softly.

The breeze scattered more rose petals on the ground as she walked to the end of the lawn.

*

Fifty years. Half a century. She didn't feel any different yet things seemed to change in her head, like a wheel turning slowly and heavily through a muddy path. She stood quietly and looked at the hills beyond the garden. The sun was covered by a huge dark grey, elephant-shaped cloud that moved gradually to the north. It was sure to rain tonight, she thought absentmindedly, better tell the servants to cover the garden chairs, but then the sun emerged from behind the cloud and the entire garden was suddenly lit up by a startling, grey-gold light.

She was fifty today.

A faint ray of sunlight crept up and touched her feet gently, and suddenly it seemed as if her life had been returned to her.

These past years had belonged to someone else. Now, as she stood in the sudden sunlight watching the blue butterfly disappear, her lost years came back, given to her as her fiftieth birthday present.

It was then that she made up her mind.

Nimmi walked back to her room, taking care not to go past the drawing room where her mother-in-law was dozing. She opened her bedroom door gently and went in, stood for a while, then opened the top cupboard and took out a small bag. Quickly packed a few things. Her medicines, undergarments, three suits and a night-dress. She didn't take any saris or expensive shawls. She pulled an old cardigan out of the top shelf and a woollen scarf she had knitted last winter but never wore because Mohan didn't like it. She shut the bag and took a quick look around the room. There was nothing here that belonged to her, yet she felt a pang of sadness saying goodbye to the thirty years she had spent in this room.

*

She waited till after lunch when the servants went to their quarters for their long afternoon break. They would return only at five to give her mother-in-law her tea. That gave her enough time to get to the bus stop. She had a few thousand rupees with her which she hoped would be enough. She wasn't sure what things cost because she never went shopping herself. The servants bought everything and Jano paid them.

Mohan never gave her any cash. "What do you need money for? You tell Jano and he will get you whatever you want from our shops. Just make a list and give it to him – but show it to me first."

Nimmi had surreptitiously saved money from the change Mohan left on his bedside table, and some she had won at rummy at the Club. Then there was the money her brothers sent her for Rakhi and Diwali and her birthday every year. There was quite a lot now in the little silk purse she kept hidden under her shawls. Somehow she had never told Mohan about this money and now, so many years later, she realised why.

When she left the house she took the longer route down the hill in case one of the servants' children was walking about collecting firewood. The ravens called shrilly from the pine trees, as if they knew what she was doing and tried to raise an alarm. But the house stayed silent, its wooden shutters tightly shut against the afternoon sun. No one noticed that she had left.

*

Nimmi had never travelled by bus, except to go on a school picnic decades ago, and she didn't know where to buy a ticket. She knew this was the bus stand because they passed it every time they went to Simla or Delhi, their driver blowing his horn loudly as he drove through, scattering the crowd. Many people recognised Mohan and saluted, but he ignored them. Mohan didn't like crowds.

She saw one such crowd jostling at a window and walked up to it. The bag felt heavy in her hand but she didn't want to hire a coolie for such a small bag, and anyway she couldn't see one around.

"Where do I buy a ticket?" she asked a man leaning on a wooden railing. He looked up at her, his eyes glazed with alcohol, and swayed gently.

"Who knows, sister? Who knows, rich lady? Give us a coin."

Nimmi looked around as others pushed past her and went ahead. People were staring at her and a beggar-woman came up with her palms outstretched, crying in a sing-song voice. When Nimmi ignored her, she moved away, cursing under her breath. "Are you going to take it all with you?"

The drunk laughed loudly, then shook a fist at the beggar-woman.

People were buying tickets at the window but Nimmi would have to push her way through their loud voices and strange smell to get hers. She forced herself to stay calm. There was nothing to fear. All she had to do was walk through the crowd and buy a ticket to Simla, she said to herself as her heart raced with anxiety.

"You want ticket to where?" asked a small boy in English. His hair was shining with oil and stood up in spikes like a parakeet's jaunty crest. He was thin and had a scar on his forehead shaped like a plus sign.

"I want to go to Simla," she said in Hindi.

"Give me Rs. 50 and I will get you the ticket."

Nimmi looked at him, wondering what to do.

"I am not a thief, madam. I can take your bag and run if I want to, but I do not want to. I do not steal from old ladies. If you want a bus ticket I will get it for you," he said, swinging on the railing. She noticed his shoes were too big for him, that he had stuffed balls of newspaper near the heel to make them fit.

Nimmi took out her purse and counted out the money for him. She would have to take the risk otherwise she would never be able to get on the bus today. She couldn't go back to the house and face Mohan. This was her only chance, given to her once in her entire life, to do something for herself. She would have to trust the boy.

*

Later, when she got to know his name and bits of his life that he wanted to tell her, she knew she had done the right thing that morning. Govind had been sent by the gods to help her. They had watched her leave the house and had followed her to the bus stop. They knew she was incapable of doing anything for herself, so they had gently guided her to the railing where Govind waited, his jaunty crest waving like Krishna's peacock plume. He had not only bought her a bus ticket, getting her a seat right in front so that she would be comfortable, he had travelled with her, sitting next to the bus conductor at the back.

"Where did you get the bus fare from?" she asked him one day as they were digging up vegetables in the garden of Hollyhock Guest House.

"The bus conductor is a friend of mine and lets me travel free. I help him with the luggage, you know, loading and unloading it."

After she had bought her ticket, Nimmi phoned her mother from a phone booth and told her she was coming to stay.

"For how long?" her mother's voice had crackled over the phone. "Bharto has gone on leave and the 'badli' cook is terrible, steals all the sugar," she whined, her voice breaking up.

"Ma, I have left Mohan, I am coming home," Nimmi said,

surprised at how easily the words came out though it was the first time she had said them out aloud.

There was a low humming sound at the other end. Her mother had disconnected the phone.

Nimmi explained her change of plan to Govind and they got off at Solan instead. She remembered an old school friend of hers who taught at a boarding school nearby, and wrote to her often asking for donations. Surprisingly, Mohan always gave generously. "Education is a good thing. I like good education," he said as he signed the cheque.

*

It all seemed so long ago. She felt as if she had always lived in this tiny room, filled with plants and books, in one corner of Hollyhock Guest House. Mohan, his mother, the house she had lived in for thirty years, seemed to belong to another lifetime. Mohan had been eerily silent ever since he found out from her mother that she had left him. Maybe he didn't believe it and was waiting for her to turn up at the breakfast table one morning. Maybe they hadn't noticed she had left.

For some reason her father had sounded very pleased when she rang him up to tell him she was living in Solan now. "Good thing, girl," he said. "Stay down. That's my girl."

She wasn't sure whether he was talking to his favourite Labrador bitch or to her, but he had sent her a money order for five thousand rupees, so he did know where she was.

*

Nimmi hadn't realised how difficult it would be to start a new life or how ill-equipped she was to do so. Some days, when she couldn't cope, she wondered if she had done the right thing. A heavy load seemed to cling to her back at night and she would wake up crying, trying desperately to shake it off. But when the black cloud passed and her fears melted away, she was filled with such joy that she started crying all over again.

Slowly, inch by inch, she emerged like an insect from a cocoon and now she knew she could brave the dangers of a life alone, unless something terrible happened. She had to learn complicated things like getting a gas connection and filling up forms in triplicate for a ration card which she needed to open a bank account.

"Your husband's signature here," said the clerk.

Nimmi looked at him blankly.

"If widow, put father's signature," he said peering at her through the bars on his tiny window. He had a big black mole on his cheek.

Nimmi just scribbled some name, which seemed to work, and she now had a bank account with hardly any money in it. She had a place to stay at the Hollyhock Guest House but she would have to find work soon.

When she arrived in Solan, her friend Shanta had been very pleased to see her and invited her to stay with her. "I have lots of room and you will love the garden." But when she heard that Nimmi had left Mohan she became a bit distant and cold.

"Are you sure you've done the right thing, Nimmi? It isn't easy in this country to be a single woman, and at your age, too. You're not qualified to do anything much," she added, shaking her head and throwing her a pitiful glance.

What she didn't say was that Nimmi had never done anything in her life except to cut fruit or arrange a few flowers when people came to dinner.

After two weeks with Shanta she moved to the Hollyhock Guest House at the end of the road. It was shabby and old, but the room was quite cheap and there was a big rambling garden behind the house. Govind had worked once for the elderly couple who ran the guest house, washing dishes and running errands.

"First we get a room and later we will ask them if you can do some work here, madam. Maybe first we ask for job and then you can get the room free. They always need people here. You can do something, can't you?" he asked, eyeing her uncertainly.

Govind kept helping her, though he went to Simla by the morning bus to work as a coolie. He always brought some fruit or a packet of biscuits back for her. Shanta didn't like him hanging around the house so he slept at the bus stand.

*

Mr. and Mrs. Sharma rose with folded hands as she came in through the gate. Their young daughter smiled at her but Mrs. Sharma told her to go in. "Welcome," said Mr. Sharma loudly. They thought she was a guest and were amazed when she asked them for a job.

"We don't know what you can do here, a lady of your class. We are just a small guest house, you know, only eight rooms, not a hotel with a coffee shop or anything," said Mr. Sharma, pulling at his tie nervously as if it was he who was asking for a job.

But they did employ her as a housekeeper and receptionist. She was to answer the phone and make sure all eight rooms were cleaned and ready for guests. It wasn't too difficult but she made many mistakes and Mrs. Sharma would shake her head at her and click her tongue. "I can see you have been doing nothing much, though half your life is over."

Govind showed her how to make the dhobi's list and how to speak to the cleaning boy so that he wouldn't answer back. "I will fix him. I know his kind well," he said before going off to Simla.

*

The guest house was quite busy even though it was the end of the summer season in the hills. "Now many honeymoon couples will come," said Mr. Sharma rubbing his hands with glee. "They pay good rates, higher than normal," he added with a wink.

Nimmi adjusted her sari (she had bought some ordinary cotton ones from the small shop in Kasauli) and rose. A group of people stood by the door looking in uncertainly. "Can I help you?" she asked.

"Yes, yes. Are you the manager here? We need three rooms," said a large man, mopping his brow. He wore a red kurta with gold buttons and seemed to be the leader of the group.

"You are lucky, we have three rooms free," said Mrs. Sharma, tucking her knitting under her arm and coming to the desk. All the rooms at the guest house were empty but they had to pretend otherwise or the guests might think it was not a popular place.

"My younger brother has just got married. We have all come

for the honeymoon, we are three brothers", he said looking back at the couple giggling outside the door.

Nimmi wrote their names down in the register. Mr. and Mrs. Gurdayal, three times, and told Govind to take them to their rooms. "We want to be next door-next door, please," said the youngest brother.

"You see, we are three brothers married to three sisters," explained the man in the red kurta. "This is your guest house?" he asked. Nimmi shook her head and looked down at the register. The man worked for Mohan in Simla and she suddenly remembered he had come to the house last month to invite them to his brother's wedding. Mohan had refused, of course, and sent an expensive gift with the driver.

What should she say if he asked her why she was here, she thought, her head spinning.

"Come on, what are you chit-chatting about?" The man's wife called him impatiently and he grinned as he sheepishly followed her out of the room. He had no idea who she was though he had seen her just a month ago. Maybe Mohan wouldn't recognise her either, would walk past her if she ever went home.

As soon as the honeymoon couple and their family had been settled in their rooms, another party arrived – an old couple breaking journey on their way to Delhi – and Mr. Sharma greeted them like old friends. Suddenly the guest house was bustling with noise and Govind turned up once more to help with the dishes. They only served breakfast, and if the guests wanted they could order food from the restaurant next door run by Mrs. Sharma's nephew.

"Who is she?" Nimmi heard him ask as soon as she had left the room.

"We don't know. She adds class to our guest house, Mr. Sharma says, but I'm not sure. A woman on her own…" replied Mrs. Sharma and then began to whisper.

*

Nimmi only met the English lady's ghost once but heard her often at night, stomping through the garden on her white horse. At first she thought it was Mrs. Sharma's daughter who was a bit slow and padded around the garden singing loudly to herself. "Soft in the head," Mohan would have called her but Nimmi often sat and played with her when they were in the garden. Mrs. Sharma watched them, her eyes full of suspicion, but gradually she began to leave Mala alone with Nimmi. She sat near her feet at the reception desk and tore endless bits of paper and then made them into tiny balls like Nimmi had taught her. The guests would look at her, then look away. For some reason Govind felt very shy when she was around and avoided them when they played in the garden.

The night she saw the ghost she had just finished reading to Mala and had sent her off to her parents' room down the corridor. From her window she saw the full moon suspended in the sky above the hills, the garden a pool of bright, white light. She wondered what Mohan and her mother-in-law were saying about her. Just then she saw a tall, fair woman float past. She glided to the edge of the garden, to the old deodar tree, then came back holding a horse. Both gleamed in the silvery moonlight, their outlines blurring and merging. Nimmi didn't feel afraid at all as she saw them walk past her. The woman didn't turn her head but Nimmi felt she was looking at her.

She never saw them again though she often stood near her window on full moon nights. The woman had a sad face and it seemed she wanted to say something to Nimmi. Maybe she was running away from home and needed her help. It would be difficult for her, having that horse to look after, as well.

"Never try to speak to her," said Mrs. Sharma when she told her about the English lady. "You may think you speak very good English but she will not like it," she said rolling her eyes. "Leave her alone, she only comes once a year and doesn't do us any harm. Poor thing, her fiancé abandoned her and never came back so she keeps walking around the hills looking for him. Men, I tell you, all alike, both the living and the dead."

After the honeymoon party and the old couple left, the guest house was quiet for a few days and then a group of schoolteachers arrived. Mr. Sharma was very pleased to see them but his wife greeted them coldly. "They never order food. Great misers these women are. They boil eggs in the kettle and make a mess in the rooms. Biscuit crumbs and orange peel all over the bed and carpets," she grumbled as Nimmi counted the towels and handed them to the dhobi.

"What can they do?" said Mr. Sharma, "a schoolteacher earns nothing."

"Who asked them to go for holidays, then? Let them stay at home or in a dharamsala," hissed Mrs. Sharma and slapped down a sheaf of bills on the counter.

Nimmi began sorting them out and then a noise at the door made her look up. A car had driven right up through the gate and parked almost in the flower beds. Her heart began to race and she felt a hot wave of fear rise in her. Mohan stood at the door.

"I don't care. My driver will park here!" he shouted, then turned around.

"So this is where you're hiding! Are you insane to live in a filthy place like this? Get into the car at once," he ordered, peering at her , his green eyes shining like a tiger's in the dimly lit room.

"You heard me, Nimmi, get into the car!" The curtains fluttered in the window and Nimmi knew Mr. Sharma was hiding in the dining room. Mala got up from the floor, put a ball of paper in her hand and squeezed it, then she stood staring at Mohan.

"I am waiting in the car. You better be out in five minutes. I don't like this at all!" he said and walked out of the door. Mala smiled at him and waved.

"Sahib is very angry, memsahib. Please come. Where is your bag? Or let your bag be, there is no time, I will fetch it later," said Jano looking nervously over his shoulder. Mala tried to give him a paper ball but he ignored her.

Nimmi followed him out. The bright sunlight made her squint and she peered at Mohan sitting in the car. Jano opened the door for her. Everything suddenly seemed very quiet and the sparrows, always so noisy, were watching her silently from the shade of the pine tree.

Nimmi held on to Mala's hand and said in a low voice, "I am not coming with you. I want to stay here, please let me."

"Why are we wasting time like this? Why don't you listen

to me when I tell you something? Are you deaf as well as stupid? Get into the car," he commanded looking straight ahead.

Nimmi turned around. The sparrows suddenly began to chatter. The sound was deafening and she covered her ears with her hands. Her knees began to tremble and she couldn't breathe.

Mala patted her hand. "I will make you some more paper balls, don't cry," she said and waved to the car as it drove away.

Her Own True Place

SEEMA scrubbed her hands with a piece of lemon rind, trying to get the curry smell out. She had opened the window and put the exhaust fan on, just as Robi had told her to. She tried to remember what else she was supposed to do to get rid of curry smells in the house.

"Put chimney exhaust on, open windows, wash chopping board ...," she counted them off on her fingers which now smelt of garlic and lemon juice. As she stood counting, the fragrance of a rich, spicy curry floated freely all over the house, getting into the curtains, sneaking under the carpets and creeping into the silk cushions.

Who would have thought how difficult it was to get rid of food smells. At home it never mattered, in fact, the house was always filled with cooking smells; mustard oil smoke, garlic and onions being fried, cumin seeds roasting and chapattis baking on a hot tava. It was a warm, welcoming aroma and everyone who came into the house felt happy to be engulfed by it.

"Yes! Room freshener," she remembered and opened the

kitchen cupboard to look for it. She smiled as she remembered how she had once sprayed herself with room freshener in a department store, thinking it was a free perfume sample. Robi and Nina had been quite upset with her.

*

It must have been the first week she arrived here, a few months after she had turned fifty-two and retired from her job at Bannon Girls' school. She could easily have got an extension, the headmistress had already said so, but Robi had other plans for her.

"Why do you want to keep working at your age, Masi? And for this rubbish pay. I have this huge house in London, four bedrooms and a living room, and a huge patio. Nina and I are away at work all day. You can be totally independent and not worry about money or anything. And it would be a great help to us too to have you there. Almost like having Ma with us," he said smiling at her. Her late sister's eyes twinkled at her and a voice in her head said, "Come on, my Tuktuk, say yes. Say yes to my little boy."

Her older sister had been like a mother to her. Seema was the second youngest of seven children and Badi had looked after her for as long as she could remember. She had oiled and plaited her hair every morning before school, packed her tiffin and made sure she did her homework every day. Their mother was always in the kitchen or in some remote corner of their sprawling house, and when Seema fell down and cut her knee she always came running to Badi.

She wasn't sure she wanted to move to London at her age. She had a little money saved up and could always give tuitions at home. Many of her students had already asked her to – some of the older ones who were married were very keen to bring their children to her. She didn't need much to live on so she would still have some money to travel to places. Simla, Ajanta-Ellora, Kerala ... there were so many places she wanted to see. Her little flat belonged to her thankfully; her late father had gifted it to her a few months before he died.

"I never spent any money on your wedding or dowry like your other five sisters, so this flat is yours. You can leave it to your brothers if you wish," he said and patted her head. He looked at her and shook his head. "I only wish they had studied and passed all their exams like you did. They could have used some of your brains."

There had been some resentment amongst her brothers when the Will was read out but Badi had supported her. "It was our father's wish and there should be no more talk about it. You two will have the big house after Ma goes and all the land that Babuji gave you."

Ma passed away, and then Badi after a few months. Seema couldn't remember her mother's face anymore but Badi came to sit at her bedside every night. Robi was her only child. A very bright boy who had always come first in class. Seema would help him with his homework and copied out all his notes before an important exam. She would read them out to him as he walked up and down repeating each word. Badi would watch them and smile and then go into the kitchen to make something delicious for both of them to eat.

"Brains are getting tired now. Must eat, both of you."

Now Robi was an important man, a chartered accountant

in a big firm in England, and had married a girl who was a lawyer. She was not very pretty everyone said at home, because she had a dusky skin and a snub nose, but here people called her a beauty. She was a quiet girl and at first Seema had tried to chat with her, ask her about her family back in India (she came from Chennai) but got very curt replies. Now Seema only spoke to her when she asked her a question.

"Is the laundry done?"

"Do you know where my black sweater is?"

"Please try to put less oil in the food. Robi must be careful."

*

Seema took out all the cleaning things and stood them in a row. Though she had now been in London for over a year and got used to most things in the house, the cleaning ritual never failed to amaze her. At home you had a broom with a sturdy handle tied with string, and a bucket with a pocha swimming in it. You swept the floor with the broom, the grassy stalks sometimes shedding bits of tiny seeds, and then you dipped the pocha into the water and swabbed it. That was it. Sometimes you might take a cloth duster and wave it at the glass ornaments or china figures and books to make the dust fly about a little before it settled down again with a silent sigh.

Here cleaning was a serious business, almost like giving an important exam every morning. You first had to learn the names of all the different cleaning things and what they were used for. The fine print explaining everything was always very tiny, and Seema had to put on her reading glasses and hold the bottles up to the light in order to read it.

There was a thick, green liquid with a nice lemony smell

which could only be used for dishes, then a creamy, pale green one which was meant for the bathroom but only for the sink and the tub, not the toilet. For that there were three bottles: a tiny, heart-shaped one that was hung under the rim, waiting patiently for someone to flush the toilet after which it jumped into action, spraying a strong scent of dead flowers. The fragrance was called 'Forest Glade' and had a picture of beautiful, bright pink and white blossoms, which always reminded Seema of children's fairy tales. The toilet also claimed a plain white bottle which she had to wear gloves to use because it contained bleach, and finally a little toy-like duck with an upturned brush, also for the bathroom.

Seema often wondered as she cleaned the toilet, using its various accessories, what Chintu's mother, their old sweepress at home would make of all this. Would she throw away her old broom made with fine sticks which she used in a desultory fashion and take these colourful, scented bottles to her bosom, or would she turn up her nose at them and spit like she did when Seema scolded her for not cleaning the bathroom floor properly?

The glassware had its own special liquid which made each glass sparkle as if a fairy had touched it with her wand, and the wooden floor had to be cleaned with a lovely, musk-scented polish. The four large mirrors in the house claimed their own bottle with a spray, and the windows had a similar one with a bigger nozzle. At no time should these various bottles be mixed up, Robi had warned her, though he never said what would happen if they were.

But Seema didn't want to risk anything so she always lined

them up like toy soldiers first thing in the morning after Robi and Nina had left for work.

"Now, you will come with me first," she said nodding at the bathroom cleaner. "The rest of you wait till I get back. No talking to each other or spilling over. Your turn will come one by one. Be patient."

Seema liked to hear her voice echoing in the empty house. She always spoke in Hindi, though after Nina and Robi came home they all spoke English. Not that they spoke much. The house was always quiet whether she was alone in it or there were the three of them. Robi would go to his 'den' and put the television on while Nina would change and go to the gym. Seema would be in the kitchen getting the food ready, taking care not to make too much noise with the pots and pans.

They ate separately too – Robi in the den, Nina in the drawing room, working on her computer and Seema in the kitchen at her little table – except when they had friends over. Then the long wooden table would be laid with the best plates and cutlery, wine glasses and hand-painted dishes which Seema had to wash by hand.

She never came out when they had guests. The food she had cooked was placed on a food warmer and everyone helped themselves. She only saw the guests through a half-shut door when they passed her room to go to the toilet. The women wore short dresses that showed their bare arms and legs and many of them smoked.

"Masi is a great cook, we're so lucky to have her here. Can you imagine my clever wife doing all this?" she heard Robi say, and everyone laughed. She wondered if Nina laughed too.

"See, Badi, your son likes my cooking. You always said I was a bad cook, not cutting the vegetables properly, always adding too much salt, but here in this new land I have become a great cook. They love my food and many of them ask Nina for the recipes. She says she will email them but I know she never does because she never asks me. Badi, your little Tuktuk is a famous cook now," she would laugh as she cleared the dining room the next morning while Robi and Nina slept late.

Sometimes she took the leftovers to the lady who ran the dry-cleaning shop down the road. Robi and Nina didn't know this and wouldn't have liked it.

"You should be careful who you speak to, Masi. In London one has to watch out for strange, mad people. Never look at anyone directly even if they ask you the way," she had been warned. But no one ever looked at her or asked her the way.

*

She only knew how to go to the end of the road where the shops were and to the post office. She was too scared to go beyond that safe zone though she wanted very much to visit the library which stood across the road. Robi took her every Saturday to the big supermarket to buy fish, meat and vegetables. They always had an ice cream after the shopping was done and Robi always told her not to tell Nina because he was on a diet. Once he stopped on the way and bought her a few books when she asked him to, and was surprised when she chose only a few old classics.

As she entered the shop, a bell rang and Mrs. Singh looked up, smiling. "You have again brought me nice-nice things to eat. Wait, let this 'mem' go, then we will open the box, otherwise we will have to share with this one, too. You know how they love our food," she muttered in Hindi.

So Seema perched on the wooden stool by the table cluttered with spools of thread, bits of cloth, paper patterns, scissors and boxes of darning needles, and watched Mrs. Singh deal with the customers. She loved the way the old lady spoke English with a strong Punjabi accent but with great confidence.

"No, no, Felicity, I tell you for the last time. I will not mend this dress again if you are not more careful. See the tear. It will take me one week to mend it. You pay me £20," she said to the pretty English girl who giggled and opened her purse.

"You are a real sweetie, Mrs. Singh. Thanks a ton. Could you please do it by next Tuesday?"

"Okay, okay. Bye now," said Mrs. Singh gently pushing the girl out of the shop and slamming the door shut. Then she lifted her head and shouted, "You go for lunch now, Mel." As soon as she had spoken a thin, dark boy came running down the stairs and rushed out of the shop.

"Can't wait to get his lunch, I think he is always starving, poor boy." She sat down with a sigh, kicking her shoes off. Seema opened the big plastic picnic box which had several small containers within. Both women looked at each other and smiled as the strong aroma of a one-day old curry filled the shop.

"I always say leftover curry tastes better than fresh. My mother used to cook and keep the meat curry by the kitchen stove all night and we ate it next day with hot rotis. Ahhh … the joy!" said Mrs. Singh, wiping her plate with a piece of bread. They had finished the lemon pulao and the cauliflower but there was still some kofta curry left which they ate now with bits of bread. After they had wiped the plastic container clean, Mrs. Singh unplugged the iron and put the electric kettle on to make tea. They chewed a cardamom each and spat it into their cup of tea and then shut their eyes as they inhaled the fragrance of home and their past lives.

This meal of leftovers they have together once a week makes Seema feel whole again, though she hardly knows Mrs. Singh and doesn't have much in common with her. Mrs. Singh only studied till Class VIII in her village school and then came to London with her husband who owned this shop. After he died her sons wanted to sell it but she kept it going, learning how to manage the trade on her own.

"My sons have good jobs in Dubai, big cars, big houses. But I like my little shop. It is my own and I can sit here with pride," she says each time to Seema. She is the only darning shop left on the street and has a stream of English women begging her to mend their expensive dresses. Though she's quite rude to them sometimes, calling them lazy, naughty girls, they seem to like her and often bring her little presents like chocolates and scented soap. She gives them to Seema and sometimes also gives her old magazines that her customers have left in the shop, to read.

*

The little shop is her oasis in this foreign place where she knows no one, will never find anyone she can talk to and where she can go nowhere on her own. Here, for an hour, she becomes herself again, content and sure of herself. She knows she cannot do anything wrong in this tiny, shabby shop filled with torn and soiled clothes. The freshly darned and dry-cleaned garments, enclosed in plastic, hang safely in the room upstairs where curry smells cannot reach.

One day she will go home again. She will ask Robi to buy her a ticket and she will get onto the plane and go home. Badi will understand even though Robi and Nina will not.

"You have everything here. This lovely house, garden. You can watch television all day. We will take you to the seaside one day soon when the weather improves. What do you have at home, Masi? Just noise and filth. Mamaji has rented your flat out, by the way."

A year goes by and Seema can now go to the supermarket on her own. She takes care to avoid the pub on the way because she hates the way the men look at her. She wears pants now and a long sweater from Marks & Spencer's because Nina doesn't want her to look like a Bangladeshi immigrant in her sari and shawl. She knows her way around the shops but never goes beyond the line drawn for her by Robi.

Two more years pass. She can go a bit further now, even travel by bus, but doesn't know what to do when she does go beyond the old safe zone. Sometimes she just takes the bus and goes to the end of the line and back again. She peers into the houses, tries to look through the windows but everything is shut and the people who live in them always seem to be away. The library is now within her reach and she goes there every afternoon to read and search for books, though they don't have many old classics. She tries to read bestsellers now.

She doesn't think of going home much these days though Mrs. Singh has asked her to go with her to Delhi. "I will be very happy if you travel with me, Seema. I feel scared going alone on the plane. If we buy our tickets now, we can get them very cheap. We will have fun in Delhi, eat and eat hot pakoras, jalebis, samosas and kulfi," she says, smacking her lips like a child.

Seema wants to ask Robi in the evening for some money for her ticket, but he looks angry and upset about something when he comes home. He shuts himself up in the den and she can hear him talking to someone on the phone, shouting and arguing. Nina doesn't go to the gym, she sits in the drawing room but her computer is switched off. Seema stays in the kitchen, not sure what she should do. At nine she asks Nina if she should put the food out and Nina nods, still staring at the blank computer screen.

"We have to just pack up and go to India, that's it. Pack up and leave. After all these years, go back with my tail between my legs. What a joke!" says Robi as he comes out of the den, rubbing his eyes. Nina stares at him for a minute and then switches her computer on. A happy musical tune fills the room and Robi sits down on the sofa holding his head in his hands.

"Home, we are going home!" Seema tells Mrs. Singh and they both burst out laughing for no reason. The curry they are eating today is freshly made, Seema cooked it in the morning and brought it over. Robi and Nina didn't ask her where she was going when she walked out of the house at noon with the picnic box. She seemed to have become invisible to them in the last one week as they packed and repacked, throwing out things they had collected over the years.

Seema knows now that she, too, is dispensable but her heart is filled with joy.

"Badi, I am going home! Your son is taking me home," she says as she sits down after lunch to pack her tiny suitcase. She would love to take the cleaning bottles, her old friends, home but she knows they will be of no use there. The old broom made with thin sticks was just right for her small house.

Everything in this world, however small, has its own true place, she had read somewhere long ago when she used to read a lot and now, at last, more than half a century later, she knows it's true.

The Pink Velvet Dressing Gown

NOBODY was sure when the dressing gown first came into the family. I always thought that it belonged to my grandmother but my mother said it was her eldest aunt's – a present from her nephew, a black sheep who had emigrated to Canada and married a blonde woman five years older than him. The aunt never wore it because she was sure the "mem" had chosen it. "It is tainted by that evil witch's hand and I will never touch it. She may have put a curse on it for all I know." Moreover it was a lurid shade of pink and her husband, a retired judge, thought it would make her look like a woman of the bazaar. "Which bazaar woman ever wears a dressing gown," said my mother's aunt, and my mother wondered how the uncle knew about bazaar women but she didn't say anything. Everyone in the family was in awe of the judge.

After keeping the dressing gown wrapped in its original gold embossed white plastic bag for a year, the aunt finally gave it to my mother. "You are the most modern amongst us, you may have some use for it. I don't want to give such an expensive thing to the maid. It will spoil her forever," she said throwing the packet on the bed, right in the middle of my mother and the aunts.

They sat around drinking tea and eating pakoras, and occasionally one of the older women would peer into the packet but not touch it, as if it was a living thing that would harm them. When they left the room, my sister and I sneaked in and took the dressing gown out of its shiny packet. We thought it was the most beautiful thing we had ever seen. A robe fit for a queen from a fairy tale – the gleaming pink velvet, the majestic frilled collar with its gold lace edging. It seem to light up our old house with its dark corners, sun-faded curtains and ancient furniture.

"What a silly gift to send from Canada where you get so many wonderful things. The mem could have sent woollen socks or a sweater or a thermos. That black sheep nephew must have lost his mind after marrying that old woman," my mother muttered every time she opened her wardrobe and saw the pink dressing gown peeping out like a tongue from the white plastic bag.

When I grew older I understood her anger. My mother's aunt, an energetic eighty year old, could have never worn a dressing gown because women of her generation always went to bed fully dressed in a sari, blouse and petticoat and the only time they undressed was when they bathed. In fact this aunt's younger sister almost didn't get married because the prospective groom's family were wary about bringing a girl who had been educated upto Class X into the family. "She might be the kind who wears a dressing gown and asks for bed-tea," they said, shaking their heads in disapproval. So the family had to promise that she would never to do such a thing and the word dressing gown was never mentioned, while bed-tea was always referred to as early morning tea. This family secret made the innocent gift from Canada even more unwelcome, but how was the poor woman sitting in a faraway land to know?

My mother never wore the dressing gown either, except on rare occasions when unexpected family members dropped in before she had had her bath. The dressing gown had a frilled collar edged with gold lace which pricked your skin when you wore it. My sister and I sometimes wrapped ourselves around it when we were playing make-believe games. I was always the poor servant girl and my sister the queen so I very rarely got to wear the dressing gown. But we often fought over it and once she tore a bit of the gold lace off.

As the years went by the cruel Indian heat began to affect the fabric, making the velvet shrivel up like an old piece of leather. But the collar still held itself upright like a chameleon's ruffle and when my mother wore the dressing gown, her cascading grey curls swirling around her shoulders, my father remarked that she looked like Louis XIV, especially when she stood on the balcony haggling with the vegetable hawkers on the street below. Beggars passing by would often call out to her, "O Beautiful Queen, throw us a coin. Your sons will flourish." Since she only had two girls, my mother didn't bother to throw them any.

We grew up and went away to college in another city. When we came home for the holidays, the dressing gown still lurked in my mother's wardrobe. She tried giving it away to various relatives, saying in the cajoling tones of a skilled shopkeeper that it was imported and very expensive, but no one wanted it. Somehow, over the years, the dressing gown had acquired a bad reputation and was considered an ill omen in our extended family.

My mother now wore it around the house all the time as she grew old and too tired to wear a sari. It was still very warm and cosy like an old pair of shoes, and I too used it when I came to visit her.

Gradually the dressing gown changed to suit us. As I grew older and my figure grew heavier and clumsier, the dressing gown expanded to fit my girth. The bright pink was softer now and sometimes in the morning light it looked almost mottled brown, like Europeans who have lived under the harsh Indian sun for too long. The lustrous, soft texture of the velvet changed as patches of coconut oil, sandalwood talcum powder and tiger balm stained it with a pale gold patina. The collar edged with lace aged better than us, turning from gold to gleaming silver with age.

Finally my mother gave the dressing gown to me. "You can wrap the baby in it if it's a girl," she said. She had washed it carefully at home but the fragrance of memories, happy, sad and indifferent, still clung to the fabric. My mother-in-law didn't want me to bring the pink dressing gown to the hospital because she said it would tempt fate to send us a female child instead of a much-longed for son, but I packed it in my case, anyway.

When my daughter was born I couldn't wrap her in the dressing gown because she was underweight and had to be kept in the incubator for three days. By then my mother had knitted her a fluffy pink blanket, and we both watched her all day through a glass window as she slept curled up in her pink cocoon.

I wore the dressing gown while breastfeeding my daughter and now the fabric was soaked with baby smells. My daughter grew up and the dressing gown became her favourite blanket – she would cling to it when she was upset or angry with us. My son, born a few years later, wouldn't go to sleep unless I rocked him in my arms wearing the old dressing gown.

We had to keep the dressing gown hidden high up in the wardrobe because my dog loved curling up on it whenever she found it lying around. If I tried to pull it away she would growl softly and settle herself on it more heavily. Now bits of her fur clung to the velvet and the sleeves began fraying at the edges.

Every year I thought half-heartedly of getting rid of the dressing gown and wearing one of my new ones, but my daughter protested. "Ma, you'll look like someone else!" My husband too liked its faded pinkish-brown colour and patted my back with affection when I emerged on the first day of winter in the dressing gown. "Winter is here, your mother's old dressing gown is out," he announced each year and waited for me to laugh.

My son who is so fastidious about everything, likes the bald velvet dressing gown on me though he always makes fun of it. "Here comes the circus queen," he says. I wonder if he remembers how as a child he used to cling to the dressing gown's belt and skate behind me as I walked around the house.

I knew I would never be able to throw it away. I hang on to various other things in the house which are of no use only because they belonged to people I love. My mother's old slippers, my father's jackets, my children's old shoes, my husband's torn shirts – I don't know anyone else who is as obsessed with old things. My daughter who is studying to be a doctor says I am insecure and cannot let go of my past. She says I should look ahead and get myself a hobby. "You should look beyond your family and home, Ma. Do something for yourself." I nod, but actually I don't know what she means. Where should I look? What is beyond my home? What should I do for myself? My family is my self. My husband and my son call me a clutter-bug. That I can understand. I am fifty years old and I cannot change now.

I have worn the dressing gown now for almost twenty-five years, though I have many new ones. My sister, who lives in Paris, gave me a bright pink one for my fiftieth birthday. "You need some colour now, didi, at your age," she said. She is single and slim and successful, and wears only a flimsy t-shirt to bed.

I do not know what my great-aunt or her retired judge husband would have to say if they saw her. Just as well they're all dead – my mother, my father, my aunts and their great-aunt (the original owner of the dressing gown) and her husband, the retired judge. I'm sure the black sheep nephew and his aged wife are also dead. Yet the dressing gown lives on, speaking to me every winter morning in their voices. The pink colour has disappeared except for a few patches under the arms, to remind us of its brazen origins which so shocked the retired judge. The gold lace has finally died a slow death and the frilly collar no longer stands upright and proud, giving my mother a regal air. Now it flops, tired and spent, around my heavy shoulders.

Every year at the end of winter I put the dressing gown away along with the other warm clothes, carefully spreading a handful of neem leaves over it to keep the moths away. Before I place it gently like a precious object, fragile and old, among the new sweaters and shawls, I hold it close to me for a few moments. I feel I am holding an old and trusted friend. I touch the frayed edges my children had tugged when they played hide and seek with me. I caress the once proud collar as it collapses in my hand like an injured bird. I gather the thin, faded velvet and hold it against my face. I inhale the fragrance of a life gone by – milk, talcum powder, oil and balm. I smell my children when they were young. I smell my mother when she was old. I wrap the sleeves around my neck and the old velvet feels like my own skin, faded and brown. I have to keep it forever.

Meera's Marriage

THE problem is she never got married.

Meera smiled as the words floated down and tickled her ears, raised her head and looked out of the window. Her mother and older sister were sitting outside on the veranda drinking tea, the evening sun playing hide and seek on their faces. She knew they were talking about her and leaned forward to listen. She no longer minded these endless discussions her mother and sisters had about her marital status, in fact she found it quite amusing now that she was out of any possible danger.

Meera was forty-nine now and had jumped safely out of the marriage market ring. There was no need to be on guard all the time, no danger of being paraded before nervous "boys" and their simpering women relatives. Never again would she have to wear her mother's best silk sari, borrow her married sister's gold earrings and walk into the living room with a trembling tea-tray. She would not have to answer personal questions about her weight and height and childhood illnesses. No smiling uncle would ever ask her about her "hobbies," and no sullen aunt would stare at her large feet painfully encased in one-size-smaller slippers.

Sometimes Meera felt a twinge of sadness that she hadn't got married but her sorrow wasn't for herself, it was for her parents. She felt she had let them down somehow by failing to find herself a husband. To snare a great catch like her elder sister, even an ordinary everyday husband like her younger sister's, would have pleased her parents. Her mother would have proudly announced to her relatives, "Meera is settled now. Boy is from a decent family." The relatives would immediately decode those words and understand that he was short, not at all good looking, and had lowly future prospects. Probably had a few sisters to marry off too, and had asked for a large dowry.

Meera got out of bed and reached for her dupatta. Her face stared back at her from the mirror above her bed. Though her eyes were puffy and her hair knotted untidily on top of her head, she could see that she was not too bad looking. In fact, many people thought her prettier than her sisters. Her hair, when washed and oiled, hung down to her waist like a heavy rope, and her eyes were large with a surprised look in them which gave her a young, fresh aspect even now when she was looking at fifty up close.

Her grandmother used to call her a doe-eyed beauty but always pointed to her large feet in the same breath. "You are like a peacock, my girl, all pretty feathers on the body but large ugly feet underneath. Learn to hide them. Remember always to tuck them under your sari when you sit down. Men are frightened by big feet."

Her mother would shake her head and say, "What was the use of being pretty when no man has yet found her worth marrying? A beautiful sari is no use if it finds no buyers and just sits on the shelf getting older and older." Another one of her favourite sayings was, "What will happen to this girl when we die? No husband, no children to take care of her. Where will she go in her old age? She will roam the streets like a cow who has stopped giving milk." Meera had numbered her mother's laments and would know at once which one was about to be aired.

Her sisters were short and plump with beady eyes and thin, lanky hair, yet they had a husband each, neatly tucked in their bags. They too had been displayed, prodded and questioned by the relatives but had managed to please them and were quickly married off. "God is kind. Two of them are settled well but I still have one left to go," her mother said to her father every morning at breakfast, looking at her with a worried frown like a farmer eyeing his unsold goat on market day.

"Someone will take her one day, I hope. It is not that I haven't tried. God only knows how much I tried with no help from your father. All he did was to reject, reject, reject." Her mother's voice rang out and floated down to the garden. They hadn't looked at her when she walked past them into the garden, as if she had become invisible and they remembered only her unmarried state.

The marigolds, the roses and the tulsi heard her mother's voice clearly, and later when Meera went out to water the plants, they would shake their heads in sympathy. Her beloved flowers would try to please her by bringing out an abundance of blossoms in the brightest hues. Her roses were the best in the entire colony and people often asked her for cuttings. This month she would plant a row of lettuce and tomatoes so that they could have a fresh salad every day. Her father was the only one in the house who enjoyed walking in the garden as much as she did, but he never saw her roses and sometimes trampled over the seedlings she had just planted.

"He always thought no boy was good enough for his darling daughter. Well, there she is, a bundle of joy tied around our necks. What will happen to her when we die?" her mother cried, bringing out lament number two. "Where will she go? Who will protect her? I will watch from heaven and weep but of what use will that be?" her mother moaned to visitors, and sometimes even to total strangers in the market or on the street. They would then all pause and look at Meera with wonder. She tried to look demure but often burst out laughing.

"Laugh, laugh like a jackal, my girl. One day when I am dead you will remember my words and cry."

"It is a hyena that laughs, Ma, not a jackal," said Meera.

"What do I care about these wild animals who laugh or cry when I have you hanging like a stone around my neck. You make my head ache," her mother said, pointing to the jar of Vicks near her bed.

Meera rubbed the balm gently on her mother's forehead and said, "Ma, I have a good job, I will get a pension when I retire and I can look after myself," but her mother didn't hear her, no one ever seemed to hear her. All they did was stare and shake their heads in despair.

"Meera… Meera! Please answer the phone. Still sleeping,

the princess," she heard her mother shout. She hadn't heard the phone ring at all though her mother, who was almost seventy, had. She still had very sharp ears and eyesight which picked up everything around her, but only if it had something to do with her husband or daughters. The rest of the world didn't exist for her. People could be robbed or stabbed before her eyes but she would turn away saying, "We do not know who they are. Let them deal with what fate has handed them." But if a leaf fell on her daughter's head she would shake her fist at the tree and shout. Meera knew her mother was like a tigeress and would kill for her or her sisters, but a tigress did not fret about getting her cubs married. She fed them, protected them, and then let them roam free. Her mother would never let her out of her sight as long as she lived unless she found herself a husband to get attached to.

How strange that she hadn't heard the phone ring at all. Maybe she was getting a bit deaf. Should she go for a check-up? But if she told her mother she would sigh and say, "The problem is you didn't get married." Every illness or bit of bad luck that fell upon her, however small, was blamed on her unmarried status. The other day when her car broke down just near the gate her mother had said. "If only you had got married to a husband who had a new car."

Once she was fifty she hoped her mother would stop lamenting and find something else to worry about. Her father was always buried in his books and absentmindedly asked her how was she doing in college whenever he saw her. Her two older married sisters lived nearby but they dropped in often to spend all day on the veranda of their old home. Sheela, the eldest, had married a very wealthy man who had all kinds of imaginary illnesses, so she would tell him she was going to the chemist to fetch his medicines and stop over every day to escape his incessant demands. Her other sister, Neera, had married a travelling salesman who was always away. When he was at home they fought incessantly so she often came back carrying a small suitcase and her two year old son. Meera loved the little boy and they spent all day exploring the garden while Neera sobbed and drank tea with her mother.

Though Neera and Sheela were paraded proudly by their mother in front of visitors, they never said anything to her about getting married. In fact she sometimes caught them looking at her with envy when she got up late on Sundays and spent the morning oiling her hair or roaming around lazily in the garden. Meera's hair was still black while her two sisters had greyed already. This is what marriage does to you, she thought, when combing her hair. Makes you lie, cry, turns your hair grey, yet everyone is so happy when you are safely married off. "A woman alone is a dangerous thing. She must go from her father's house to her husband's to her son's. So find yourself a husband, girl, any husband will do as long as he is alive and belongs to our caste," her grandmother would say, patting her cheeks. "See, still quite plump and nice. Not too late to grab some widower but make sure he doesn't have a string of brats."

Meera ran to get the phone. No one spoke when she answered and then a faint voice came through. It was a man with a strange accent she couldn't place. "Yes, this is Dr. Sen's residence. No, he is not at home. May I know who's calling?"

Meera wrote down the person's name and number. Ashutosh Chowdhary. Sounded like a hero in a classic novel, she thought and went back to her room. Her mother was now talking about her stomach ailments. Her sister was reading her son's comic book and Meera knew it was safe to go out and sit with them.

When Ashutosh Chowdhary arrived Meera was in the garden weeding the lawn. It was late afternoon and the sunlight fell in patches over the garden. A sudden shower had made hundreds of tiny weeds spring up and she dug them out quickly before they sank their roots deep into the earth. The mali watched her from the shade of the neem tree. She knew he didn't like her working in the garden but she just ignored his sullen looks. She felt sorry for the weeds as she pulled them out and threw them on the rubbish heap to burn. Poor things, they too needed some soil to grow in. It was not their fault they liked her lawn. Maybe she should just allow them to take over the green grass. After all they were green too, in fact a brighter green than the true grass. But people liked a green lawn with no weeds. And one had to do what people liked or you wouldn't belong anywhere, like the poor weeds.

Meera looked up and saw her father walking towards her with a stranger. She moved quietly towards the shrubs but the mali seized the opportunity to betray her by loudly calling out, "Sahib, Babyji is here." Her father, who hadn't come out to look for her, stared at her as if he had no idea who she was. The stranger too looked at her with polite interest. "Err ... this is ..." her father said, trying to remember her name. The stranger thought he had forgotten *his* name and came forward. "I am Ashutosh ... you must be Miss Sen ... Pleased to meet you. You have a lovely garden. I have never seen such beautiful roses and such unusual colours." Meera could tell the man was a charmer.

Over the years she had classified men into various categories, began doing it when they first came to 'see' her. It took just a few seconds for her to place these suitors into a labelled box. There were charmers, show-offs, shy ones, sly ones, mean ones, yes-Ma ones and dull, fish-eyed ones.

"Yes ... we do have a garden, always been here, it seems. Meera loves the plants ... yes ... this is Meera ... our daughter." Her father said, suddenly recognising her as his own flesh and blood. "So, as I was saying, the manuscript is in good shape with only a few pages missing, but it needs ..." the two men strolled to the far end of the garden and Meera rose and went into the house. She could sense her mother's excitement even before she stepped into the veranda. The house trembled and moaned like a giant waking from sleep and the curtains flapped madly in the breeze.

"Oh, Krishna in heaven ... Oh, Ma Durga ... Bless us all ... You have sent us a perfect specimen ... Not too old but not too young, either. Good height, though a bit thin. No ... I am not ungrateful, my devi, not for a moment. I accept him ... Oh, my gods ... you have come to our rescue at last," she said with her eyes shut tight and her hands fluttering on her heart.

"Ma ... please ... he might hear you," whispered Meera.

"Let him hear, let the whole world hear my heart's cry!" said her mother, shaking her head from side to side as if she was swaying to music.

"Ma, please be calm. I am sure he's married, and anyway

I'm too old, I'm going to be fifty soon," Meera said, rubbing her mother's back to soothe her. It helped sometimes to calm her down but today she was like a woman possessed. Maybe she should run and fetch the jar of Vicks.

"Our last chance! Don't you see, this is our last chance," she cried, pulling at her hair. She looked like a baby sparrow with ruffled feathers. Meera wanted to laugh but her mother looked so distraught she kept quiet.

"Anyway, you don't look a day over forty if you stand in dim light. We must dim all the lights in the drawing room at once! Tell the servants to fuse one immediately. Go, put on your pink sari … Oh … be quick! We mustn't let him get away … this, my child, could be a gift from the gods … Oh, Ma, bless us … give him to us … I am sure he is not married … he has that carefree look and he is so thin. Bless the gods! On a platter they have sent him. He is ours to take."

In the dim light of the drawing room, her pink sari glowed like a faded rose. Meera twisted her handkerchief and listened to Ashutosh's smooth voice as it floated over the room. Her mother stared at him like a fox desperately trying to mesmerise a rabbit, and Meera thought she would jump up and clamp him in her jaws at any moment. Her tiny pink tongue darted out once or twice and Meera wanted to run and hide. Her father looked around in his usual vague way and kept asking why the lights were so dim. "Must be the voltage fluctuation," he muttered. Her sisters watched him from the sofa like two wary guard dogs, waiting to pounce on him in case he tried to get away.

Ashutosh seemed oblivious of the lasso being thrown

around his neck, and did and said all the right things as he ate and drank tea non-stop. Munching on a samosa he praised the roses in the garden once more, admired the silk paintings her sisters had made when they were girls, took two generous helpings of halwa and listened politely to her mother as she listed Meera's virtues. Once in a while, as he chewed thoughtfully, he would look at her and smile.

Meera ignored him. Over the years she had learned to switch off when she was paraded like this. She would amuse herself by examining all the relatives' feet since she had to look demure and it was rude to stare at their faces. She was quite an expert at feet and voices by now. But today, for the first time, she felt embarrassed and irritated by her mother. Maybe because the 'seeing' had come after a long gap. Why must she be subjected to this humiliation now? She was almost fifty and she had no desire to get married. It was high time her mother realised this. Meera didn't care anymore, however much it upset her. She had had enough.

Suddenly, just when her mother told her to bring in the tea-tray, Meera rose. "I will not bring the tea-tray. I never bring it in, Shambhu does. So why should I do it today?" she declared and turned to the stranger. "I'm sorry you have been subjected to this, I have no wish to marry you or anyone. You may already be married, for all I know. I am almost fifty years old and very content with my unmarried status. I have a job with a good pension when I retire. I have a car and I do not need a husband at all. I would rather get a dog."

The room swirled with shocked silence. Her mother fell back on the sofa as if someone had slapped her. Her sisters giggled nervously and then fell silent. Her father muttered, "Why are the lights so dim ..." and Ashutosh burst out laughing. "Well said! I admire you for your frankness. Actually, I'm not married either and have no wish to be. Please, have no fear. I am very happy being a bachelor for life. I must say, these rasgullas are really good, did you make them?" He looked at her with an amused glint in his eyes.

"Well, I did make them and the halwa, too," Meera said a bit shyly, but she felt so much better now as if a load had been lifted from her shoulders, as if someone had untied her and set her free. Why hadn't she done this a long time ago? It felt so good.

She looked at her mother who was still slumped on the sofa, fanning herself with her sari. Meera went to the end of the room and switched on a few more lights and her father smiled at everyone. "Ah ... some brightness at last. Someone must have complained to the power station about the low voltage," he muttered and left the room.

A heavy silence fell, and as her mother sighed and began to complain about a stomach ache, Meera stood up. "I want to ask you something," said Ashutosh as he followed her out of the room. "I have tried to grow that purple rose but failed. Do you prune them early or late? Will you show me the exact place on the stem where you cut to graft ..."

Meera walked down the steps with him into the garden. Though the sun had set there was still enough light to see the roses. They smiled and nodded, glimmering in the fading light. Behind her she could hear her mother chant, "Gift him to us, O devi ... give him to us ..."

Freedom at Fifty

RANO couldn't believe the old lady was dead. She was ninety and had a bad heart and everyone, including her, knew she would die soon. But still Rano couldn't believe it. For years the old lady had been saying she was going to die. "My poor heart, it can go off any day and then you'll all be sorry." Rano could hear her whining voice saying the same words over and over again even now, and saw her thin, harsh face hover close to her.

For more than thirty-five years this shrill cry had woken her every morning, and Bibiji's bony, crooked fingers had jabbed at her every night before she fell asleep. "Press harder, you lazy wretch, press harder."

Everyone in the colony called Rano the 'martyr' and laughing, shook their heads at her. "Why do you put up with her abuses, her endless demands?" they asked but Rano just kept silent. She couldn't tell them that she did it because she loved her husband, and the old woman, however cruel and abusive, was his mother. "My beloved mother is a saint," he said to her every night before he fell asleep. Her arms still aching from pressing the old lady's feet and massaging oil on her balding scalp, Rano would nod, turning her face away. This was her life as God had written it.

Now the old lady was dead and Rano couldn't see ahead. It was strange how her arms still ached, though she hadn't done any chores for days now. She stared blankly at the huge photograph of the old lady with its small brass plate declaring her to be Neeladevi, wife of late Madhavchand, Police Inspector, retd. Bhavnapur. Rajan had had the photograph framed in a gilt-edged metallic frame and hung it near the doorway of the puja room. Rano would drape it with fresh marigold garlands every morning, light an incense stick and pray, but for the last one week she had stopped doing that and now the marigold garland drooped sadly, dry and faded. Rajan complained once or twice but she pretended not to hear him. They had floated his mother's ashes in the Ganga and carried out all the rituals the old lady had written down for them. Rajan and she had followed every little instruction in the school copybook she had handed them almost ten years earlier when she had decided she was going to die. "My heart is so frail. I may go anytime, just like that," she said often, usually after her afternoon nap, snapping her thin fingers. They had even cooked the vegetarian, no-cereal, no-chilli, no-oil meals she had ordered them to for twenty-one days. Each time she cooked the gruel, stirring it with a heavy hand, Rano heard Bibiji's high-pitched voice echoing in the kitchen. "Stir, stir properly, you lazy fool, you'll burn it. What is the matter with you, girl? Is your head full of cowdung? Your entire family is buffalo-minded."

Today was the twenty-second day, and suddenly she remembered it was also her fiftieth birthday.

No one else remembered it. Not her daughter who was in college, nor her son who was married and lived in Mumbai. Rajan, of course, never remembered and always looked upset when she reminded him, as if it was something they should all forget. For some strange reason it was the old lady who always remembered. "Today you are one year older. Remember, old age comes to everyone. Do not think you will be young forever. You skin will sag and your hair will fall out. This plait swinging on your back will become a rat's tail," she would say wagging her claw-like fingers. "Now, go fetch my teeth, but first rinse them properly."

All day Rano fetched and carried, cooked and fed, washed, combed and powered, oiled and cajoled the old lady. Though they had two maids and a young boy for all the housework, her mother-in-law insisted that Rano do all her personal chores as well as cook her meals. "Your father said you were a good cook, but I have yet to taste a single proper dish made by you," she would say, finishing all the food on her plate. Rano got up at dawn, bathed and then made tea for her mother-in-law. Then she laid her clothes out, oiled her hair and prepared her bath. She waited outside the bathroom door, in case Bibiji called out for her which she often did. "Fetch another soap – I do not like this one … The water isn't hot … there is an ant here … scrub my foot, girl, don't just stand there like like a dumb fool." When she came out of the bathroom, Rano would help her tie her sari, making sure the pleats were straight or else the old lady would rap her on the head with her knuckles. She would comb her thinning hair and tie it in a bun, and then they would sit down to pray. One hour of chanting softly so that Rajan wouldn't wake up, and then Rano would go to the kitchen to make breakfast.

After Rajan left for work, she would sit down to read the Gita to the old lady and then press her legs till she fell asleep. During that short catnap time Rano washed and ironed and made lunch for her. Often the maids would try to help but Rano refused. "She will find out and then we will all be punished."

Bibiji had a habit of raising her head, twitching her nose to sniff out where Rano had made a mistake. A crease in her blouse, a tiny stone in her rice or a speck of dust on the shelf would bring the household down. Neighbours came out to watch and children stood still as Bibiji screamed at Rano, sometimes hitting her and pulling her hair. Rajan, as soon as he came back from the office, would be told about Rano's misconduct and then she would be summoned. Her daughter looked bored, the maids sad, Rajan irritated, while the old lady, eyes sparkling, would sit in judgement and list her faults. Her past mistakes would be brought up, one by one, and new ones added. "Can you please try, for my sake," he would whisper later in the safety of darkness. "She is so old and frail. She can die any day and then we will be sorry. She will watch us from heaven and we will not be able to make any amends."

She did die finally, twenty odd years later, and now Rano couldn't believe it. She kept going to her bedroom to make sure the bed was made. She opened the old lady's almirah and refolded her clothes. She would wake up suddenly at night, panic-stricken, thinking she hadn't made her breakfast or heated the water for her bath, and then realise with a shock that the old lady wasn't with them anymore. She was watching them from heaven.

Rano didn't know what to do with the sudden freedom that overwhelmed her. She felt like a prisoner who missed his life in jail. She woke at dawn as usual and bathed, but after that she didn't know what to do. "Why do you have to wake up so early, Ma," her daughter grumbled, "just relax."

She was seventeen when she had first come to this house, a silly giggling girl who wore red ribbons in her hair. Bibiji had made her take them off at once and told her to tie her hair in a tight plait. Slowly, day by day, Bibiji drained her spirit and by the time she was nineteen she had been fully reined in by the old lady. "See my daughter-in-law, how meek she is. Not a squeak out of her ever. You will never hear a word, no matter how much work she's asked to do. Now recite the prayer I taught you yesterday, girl!" she would say, pointing to Rano as if she was a trained monkey.

Rajan was working abroad then and only came back after three years. By that time Rano was a mute girl of twenty who jumped if anyone spoke loudly to her.

She looked at Bibiji's photo now and saw her own face in the glass. She was fifty today but still looked like a young girl. Her eyes stared back at her, as innocent as a child's, and her slender body seemed to leap out of the photograph. Rano touched her face and a strange thought came to her. She stood still, but her face in the reflection kept moving as if it had a life of its own. She knew now it was her old self from a long time ago. She had remained frozen in time because the old lady hadn't let her grow. She had been stunted, her limbs tied down for three decades or more, but now she was a seventeen year old girl again. Bibiji had died and she had been reborn.

Her life had suddenly been handed back to her even though she hadn't asked for it. Rano slapped her cheeks and laughed. Her reflection laughed too, but louder. How easy it was to laugh! She called out her own name and it bounced back at her from the walls. She called out over and over again, shattering the stillness of the empty house.

*

"What are you wearing, Ma," asked Tara looking up from her book.

"Oh, just a salwar kameez I bought yesterday."

"But such a bright pink! Surely at your age … don't you think?" said Rajan, looking up sharply.

"Why not? Why not pink? Who says I cannot wear pink at my age," replied Rano, her breath coming fast. "So many other women wear pink, they even wear jeans." She had never spoken like this before to anyone, let alone her beloved husband whom she should worship. She would wear pink, bright red and maybe even crimson, and no one could stop her. She was not a widow! She wouldn't go as far as wearing jeans but she would buy new clothes, some make-up, and do whatever she wanted. She was free now. Tomorrow she was going to the cinema with her neighbour and before that they would have lunch in a restaurant. She would be back late, the maid would give Rajan his tea. She announced all this quickly and swept out of the room, Rajan and Tara's shocked, sullen silence following her like a dark cloud. Bibiji's photograph trembled, scattering a few dried marigold petals.

I cannot believe this is happening. My sweet, cow-like Rano whom I adored has changed into a witch. My Sati-Savitri … where is she? A pink salwar kameeze-wearing, cinema-going witch! Thank God, Bibiji is dead. She would be horrified by this behaviour. A pious, godfearing daughter-in-law, a dutiful wife and mother … where has she gone? Maybe it is menopause. I read in one of the women's magazines that Tara reads all the time, that women turn odd at fifty. But my Rano, so well trained by my beloved mother. Maybe I should take her to a doctor. But what will I say? What ailment does she suffer from? I can't say, "Doctor, my wife has suddenly changed into a young girl and started laughing and talking back. Her eyes sparkle and her skin glows. She's threatening to wear jeans. Please cure her. Save her from herself." But what can a doctor do? Oh, Ma, please tell me what to do. Why is Rano behaving like this? She must be over fifty now, after all I am sixty-three. She should be praying, going to the temple and cooking simple, nutritious meals for me like she's always done for you. No chilli, no oil. Duty to her husband should be the most important thing in her life, now that her son has grown up and gone away and you are in heaven. We still have a daughter to marry off. Instead she turns into a silly girl.

*

Rano combed her short hair with her new hairbrush and put on her dangling silver earrings. She had bought them yesterday after lunch. Her neighbour Sumi, who had lived next door for twenty years but whom she had only recently come to know (since Bibiji never allowed her to talk anyone outside the house) had taken her to this tiny silver shop. Rano was so excited she couldn't choose so Sumi had finally picked these ones out.

For years Rano had wanted to wear silver earrings but Bibiji said they were for servants, not bahus of wealthy families like theirs. So many things were taboo. Spicy street food, filmi music, glass bangles, short hair, magazines, nail polish, dogs, talking to outsiders, travelling alone, and wearing loud-coloured saris – crimson, red, pink or orange. Bibiji allowed only yellow, pale pink or blue, and *no* salwar kameezes.

Rano smiled at her reflection in the glass. How pretty she looked with short hair and earrings. People now said she looked like Tara's sister instead of her mother. Tara didn't like it one bit and neither did Rajan. In fact, ever since she had cut her hair he hadn't spoken to her. At the hairdresser's Rano too had felt a pang of regret when she saw her hair cascading down onto the white tiled floor. Above the loud voices and film music of the salon she heard Bibiji's angry voice, "What are you doing, you idiot girl! Only men and eunuchs have short hair. In our family no woman has ever cut her hair. I will wring your neck, you slut!" The scissors snipped but the noise couldn't drown the old lady's shrill voice. Rano's head began to ache.

Ma, she has cut her hair. Her beautiful long hair with no grey in it. You taught her to oil and plait it so tightly that not a single strand escaped, and now she has cut it! She looks like a boy. Is she punishing me for something I did? I have tried so hard to be the ideal husband, like you taught me. I bought her gold chains when our son was born, gave her money to do a puja for him. I took all of you to Badrinath for darshan. She was quite happy to stay back and look after you while I took the children up to see the snow.

She didn't mind when you asked her to do all the cleaning after you threw the servant out. You said she liked cooking, washing and ironing for you. "She will be blessed by the gods for her seva," you said. I have always asked you if she was happy and you said, "Yes, my son. Her life is full of joy because she is your wife. She worships you." Then why did she cut her hair? I wouldn't mind if she had shaved her head, I could tell people she had been to Tirupati and everyone would have respected her. But this funny boyish hairstyle?What will people say? She has made me a laughing stock in the colony! I can see the neighbours pointing to me and laughing. All this is happening because you have left us, Ma. Without you we can't control her. First movies, then lunch, then haircut! God knows what will happen next. I heard her say she wants to learn how to drive! I can't bear it. Call me to you, Ma. There is nothing left for me on this earth now.

*

Rano parked the car carefully and got out. She was still not very confident and always took either Tara or Sumi with her. She hadn't realised though that driving would be so easy. At first their driver was hesitant, but when she said she would go to a driving school, he let her sit in the driving seat. A month later she had got her license – with a small bribe, of course. Tara looked at her with sudden respect. "Well done, Ma, never thought you had it in you," she said. Rano suddenly wanted to cry but hugged her daughter instead and laughed.

"Always respect yourself. Promise me that. Whatever people say or do to you, please be honest to yourself. Don't let life take away your self," she whispered into Tara's hair.

"Why are you giving me this lecture?" said Tara and shrugged her off.

Rano walked into the house. Rajan was asleep on the sofa in the TV room. His spectacles had fallen to the ground and she picked them up. They hadn't spoken to each other for a month. Ever since the old lady had died Rajan had become like a lost child, whimpering in the shadows. Sometimes shouting angrily at nothing and then sitting and staring at the wall for hours. She knew he missed his mother terribly. She loved him, not like she had done before, blindly, but with a more honest, quiet love. She wanted to help him but something held her back. She had just been set free and was soaring high now. If she reached out to him she knew he would pull her down. Then she would sink to the ground once more and not be able to get up. Wouldn't get another chance to be free. She would help him but slowly, at her own pace. She had just learnt to walk herself, she couldn't help him till her own feet were steady. She saw the deep lines on his forehead as he slept, snoring gently. He looked angry even when he was asleep. It was she who had made him look this that and she wanted to caress his face, soothe the frown away.

Bibiji too looked angry, it seemed she would jump out of

the photograph and hit her, shattering the glass. Suddenly Rano began to giggle. She couldn't stop, her loud laughter filled the room and flew out into the street. People passing by stopped to listen but Rajan slept on. Then her eyes filled with tears. She sat down exhausted in front of the photograph and began to sob. She cried till her heart was empty of hate and sadness. She knew she was crying for all those lost years of her life. 17...24...31...45...50... She had never been allowed to be young. Now that she was standing at the brink of fifty, looking anxiously towards old age, she knew she had to reach out and catch her youth. There was not much time left. She must hurry to catch herself. Run fast – but where could she go? She mustn't go wild with this newfound freedom. She would fly off the cliff if she ran too fast, crash to the ground if she flew too high.

Balance, she needed a balance. Rano lifted her arms high above her head and then twirled around for no reason.

"No, no, be still," she said, clutching her hands. She would stay where she was and be happy to be here. Be who she was, content. Now at last she was learning to be friends with herself. She wasn't going to do things just to please her husband or to displease Bibiji. She would do what made her happy, but find out first *what* made her happy. She would have to stay very still and read herself, look at her thoughts after carefully separating them from all the clutter she had gathered over the years. There was a corner far inside her head where she had been storing things and now she would take them out, one by one, and examine them. As you did with winter clothes, you shook them out and examined them.

She looked at her reflection and saw that she suddenly seemed much older, as if someone had erased her glowing skin and sparkling eyes and put a faded face on her. But it was a wise face with laughter lines around the eyes. Her real face. Then she looked up at the photograph. Bibiji was staring at her. Slowly and hesitantly Rano smiled at her. "You and I, now we know each other. It's a pity you have gone, otherwise we could have had fun fighting, thinking up new ways to get even with each other. See, I am a different woman now, I can stand up to you. I am your equal. Maybe that is what you wanted, a woman who would fight back, a woman with spirit. I could give you a good fight now, Bibiji," Rano said and laughed.

She glanced up and saw that Bibiji was smiling back at her.

Fifty Phobia

MALTI clenched her buttocks, hoping she could keep the rising fart inside her from escaping. The girl spread the hot wax on her thighs and sighed loudly for no reason. She was new, not her old faithful Rosy who had such a gentle touch that even bikini waxing didn't hurt. She plucked eyebrows and threaded upper lips as if waving a magic wand to make facial hair disappear.

"Your hair growth is less … it happens with age," said the girl showing her a few forlorn-looking hairs embedded on a strip of nylon they now used for waxing.

"Well, I need to wax, my legs feel unclean if I don't," said Malti curtly. "Anyway it's none of your business, just get on with it and try not to pull so hard."

Malti wiggled her freshly pedicured feet, noticing that the girl shrugged her shoulders sullenly in the way these sort of girls had, and then began speading more hot wax on her leg.

I must complain about her to Rosy, she needs to learn some manners. Stupid creature, thought Malti looking at her reflection in the mirror. Their eyes met. "Your roots need retouching ... again ... so quick. Hair on legs grow slow, slow but hair on head going white very quick, very quick," said the girl and smiled, her young eyes brimming with glee and revenge.

*

Malti called the driver on her cellphone, taking care not to get her freshly painted nails smudged. She would go home, eat her lunch – salad and yoghurt – and take a short nap. A strong aroma of freshly fried samosas rose in the air from the shop next to the beauty parlour and Malti's mouth filled with the forbidden taste of the hot, spicy snack dipped in mint chutney. She swallowed quickly and looked away. Must carry some cucumber and carrot slices with me, she thought, banishing the image of a glistening, chutney-dripping samosa from her mind.

She had read somewhere that if you thought only about good low carb, low fat and low sugar food all the time, you could lose weight just like that. "Power of Good Food Thought Diet," it was called. Think salad, think cottage cheese, think yoghurt, she repeated over and over again.

The house was silent as she walked in. The part-time maid had cleaned up and gone, leaving behind a faint scent of pine and soap. The cook was dozing in the kitchen. He knew her salad, wrapped in cling film, was waiting for her in the fridge. "Anything else, memsahib," he asked quickly, getting up as she closed the fridge door with a bang.

Lazy man, did nothing but eat and sleep all day. He was getting fatter and fatter, gorging on the food that he cooked and she didn't eat. Tutu, of course, wanted a full meal for dinner so the fridge had to be well stocked. It was torture to open it and see all the butter, cream cheese, chocolates and rich, greasy curries on the shelves, mocking her. Once she was quite sure a bowl of chocolate ice cream gleaming with fudge had winked at her and she had almost reached for it, but then the Good Food Thought helped her overcome the crisis.

She would get her own fridge. Yes, why hadn't she thought of that earlier? A small fridge where she would keep her diet cokes, chopped cucumber, celery, carrots and bean sprouts. Her steamed veggies and boiled chicken would stay fresh and uncontaminated by Tutu's unhealthy, oil-rich, fattening food. Their evil aroma would not mingle with her fresh, clean, GOOD food.

She had reached this ideal size zero (well almost size zero, her bones were heavy) weight with a lot of difficulty and she didn't want to add even an inch to it. After her menopause she had to be very wary all the time about inches creeping up around her hips, waist and tummy. It was so difficult to stay thin, especially with temptation lurking in every corner of the house. Neither her daughter, Tanya nor her husband, Tutu cared about what they ate or how much weight they put on. Both ate like pigs and talked about food all the time. Tanya was twenty-five and already looked about thirty with her plump face and large hips. Her face was still young, of course, but when they went out people thought they were sisters. Malti pretended to be surprised but she loved it, though she knew it made Tanya more sullen than ever.

"Why can't you dress like other mothers, other women your

age?" she said to her, frowning. Malti was wearing skinny jeans and a cute little tank top she had picked up from GAP the other day. The shoulders hung down from one side so that your bra strap could show. The salesgirl said it really suited her though it was their new range for teenagers.

"Why should I, sweetie-pie?" she replied. "Why should I dress like an aunty when I look so good in these jeans!" The new diet was really working and her hips were as slim as a boy's. She was a bit worried about her neck, though. All this weight loss seemed to pull and tug at the skin of her neck and she was often startled to see how it sagged. Maybe it was time for a bit of nip-and-tuck. Just a little tightening of the face and a tiny dash of botox on her cheeks. The rest of her was fine. More than fine. When she walked into a room all the young men stared at her, while their wives looked at her with half-closed, envious eyes. It gave her such a thrill. Not that she wanted to have an affair with any one of them – all that love-shove was so messy and added years to your face. All she wanted was for people to look at her with that glazed, admiring look till the day she died.

Let Tanya grumble and sulk. Why should she dress like other women her age? She was slim and supple and there were no crow's feet around her eyes. She didn't look a day over thirty-five in dim light. Sometimes, in the mornings her eyes were a bit puffy and her chin sagged, but after a massage with the new placenta and caviar rejuvenating face serum (bloody expensive but worth every dollar) and oxygen mask she was ready to face the world. No one would believe she was going to be fifty in three days. Even she herself didn't believe it and was quite sure her mother, whose absentmindedness was legendary in the family, had got the year of her birth wrong. Yes, she must have.

Tutu looked his age – fifty-nine–and was quite irritatingly content to do so. "I'm middle-aged and loving it," he said patting his paunch in a vulgar way whenever she scolded him for putting on weight around his waist. Fortunately he still had all his hair and didn't look *too* old, though strangers often thought he was her father. Tutu didn't mind that and laughed each time it happened. This always pleased her no end but she made sure she looked surprised and cast her eyes down demurely to hide her pleasure.

Her own hair was thinning a bit but she had had it bonded when she was in London and now it hung thickly around her face. She coloured it very carefully, mixing three shades so that it didn't look jet black like a crow's wing, like all the other women her age. Just the other day at the Club this young man, must have been around thirty, had tried to make a pass at her. She told him off at once, but it was quite amusing since he was one of Tanya's friends. It was such a joke and when she told everyone at dinner that night they all laughed and said, "Well, when you look like a girl you have to fend off these young men." Tanya just glared at her for no reason. She wished her daughter would try to make herself a little attractive. Smile a little, flirt a little. Unfortunately she looked like Tutu's side of the family – plump and dark.

Malti was beautiful and had known that from the time she was a young girl. Everyone remarked on her looks. The family, the servants and even total strangers would stop her mother on the road and say, "She's so beautiful, may the evil eye never fall on her." Sometimes her mother made her wear old frocks so that people wouldn't notice her so much. "They might kidnap her," she would say. "What nonsense! You might leave her behind somewhere, more likely," her father would reply. He was the only one who never remarked on her good looks and often scolded her for staring at the mirror all the time.

*

Malti had made a brilliant match. Tutu was the only son of one of the wealthiest families in Delhi. Their money was old, their property and farms still intact and they were related to everyone worth knowing in the country. The men in their family were famous for their ugliness and took great pride in it. "My great-grandfather would frighten our horses, he was so ugly."

Malti was married at twenty-one and came to live in this lovely old house with ten empty rooms, except for the one where her bedridden mother-in-law lived. She had been a famous beauty in her day and now lay, white as a sheet, staring at the ceiling, muttering the names of all the people she had known to herself.

Malti visited her every morning for half an hour and then began her exercise regimen. Since Tutu was always away on endless business trips, she had made her own life which she didn't change even when her husband was home. "You're obsessed with this exercise thing," he said often as he lounged in bed watching his never-ending cricket or football matches on television, but she ignored him. She walked every morning from 5.30 to 6.30, then bathed and did one hour of yoga with her guruji. After that she visited her mother-in-law and had a glass of hot water with lime – no sugar– sitting by her bedside. For breakfast she ate sprouts and a bowl of yoghurt while Tutu and Tanya had fried eggs on toast or parathas. After they left she went to the gym to work out for an hour. On alternate days she did weights to tone up her biceps, abs and thighs. She came back, took a quick shower and maybe went shopping or to the beauty parlour to touch up her hair or for waxing.

Sometimes she had lunch with friends but ate before she went and only had a salad with them. They all laughed at her but she knew they envied her her slender, boyish body. But lunching out was very rare because she didn't like going out in the sun. She was very careful about getting a tan or pigmentation marks and had had large floppy hats made for herself. She was terrified of brown age spots which she knew women acquired as they aged, and often wore white cotton gloves if she had to go out in the sun.

"I don't have any spots, look!" her mother said pointing to her pale, golden skin. "I've never worn any gloves or hats in my life. I don't want to look like the British Queen," she laughed and Tutu too burst out laughing. He began calling her Your Majesty after that whenever he saw her going out with her hat and white gloves.

She didn't care what anyone said, she wasn't going to let herself go. She would stay as young as she could. Old age was a curse and she would fight it, she thought, as she rested for twenty minutes with a soothing face pack, listening to music, mostly spiritual. She had lit one of her aroma candles, ylang ylang, which cleared the air of any impure, negative energy.

She had read the other day that meditation kept your body young and she tried to do a bit, but it wasn't easy. All kinds of dark thoughts flowed into her head as soon as she closed her eyes, and one of them was a giant plate of jalebis, gleaming like a hundred evil eyes. Then, for some reason, her father who had died five years ago floated in front of her, smiling and nodding his approval, something he had never done in his life.

In the afternoon she watched television with her mother-in-law but took care to close her eyes often so that she wouldn't get wrinkles around them. Then her massage girl came and soon it was evening. She always ate at seven because that's what her dietician had told her to do. She only allowed carbs before seven, nothing after that. She put on a special night cream and then went to bed by nine, after reading something soothing and uplifting for a short while.

On rare occasions when Tutu was at home they watched a movie on DVD ".Why watch if you're going to shut your eyes all the time, darling?" he laughed. Tanya sniggered too. "Mum, why are you so afraid of getting wrinkles around your eyes, everyone does, you know. You have to age if you want to live. Or die at twenty-one," and then she made funny wrinkled eyes and Tutu collapsed laughing. "Oh, my sweet, young wife, my pretty little unwrinkled girl. Preserved like a sweet plum in wine," he crooned. "But no wrinkles, no no … "

*

It wasn't funny. Getting old was no laughing matter. It was frightening and Malti couldn't bear to think about it. She would rather die than be like those fat, old women with grey hair and puffy faces. No one looked at old women, they could be part of the furniture. You became invisible. Old men were fine, seemed to do quite well, in fact, going all over the place and even having affairs with young girls. Of course there were many old women, like her mother, who seemed quite happy and enjoyed their ugly bodies and wrinkled faces. "God gives us these extra years and we must be thankful. He will call us any day but till then we can enjoy life, be happy," she said every morning. How could you enjoy life when you had to look at your lined, sagging face in the mirror every morning? She would never allow herself to become like them, Malti thought, as she began doing her chin exercises. Counting backwards from fifty and breathing with her cheeks puffed out at each count. Maybe she should go for that nip-and-tuck tomorrow, not waste time letting her skin sag. Every day was crucial now. Every moment her body was plotting against her, ageing bit by bit. She patted her face gently as if reassuring an ailing child.

*

"Let's have a party for Ma's fiftieth birthday," said Tutu and Tanya clapped her hand with glee.

"Yes, yes, with big banners and all Fifties music!"

Malti looked up from her Sudoku – she did one every day, it kept the brain alert, she had read. She was also planning to learn how to play bridge on the computer, and did crossword puzzles regularly to ward off memory loss, taking care never to frown when the clues were too cryptic.

"Are you mad! I will never announce to the world that I'm fifty. Do I look fifty to you?" she demanded angrily, putting the pen down.

Her husband and daughter stared at her.

"Do I?" she shouted. They had never seen her so angry. Malti very rarely lost her temper or cried because she knew that this pumped toxins into your blood stream, but sometimes she just couldn't help herself. Rage engulfed her like a fire and she couldn't stop, however many Good Thoughts she tried to think.

"Do I look fifty to you?" she asked again, a little calmer but still flushed with anger.

They shook their head nervously. "No, you don't, sweetheart. But I just thought a party would be fun. After all you are turning fifty – a milestone, half a century, you know," he muttered, rubbing his stomach.

Malti looked at him and saw a faint glint of malice in his eyes, something she had never seen before. Tutu loved her, loved her slim figure, unlined face and firm behind. Suddenly she was afraid. She had always thought he was proud of her youthful looks, saying to their friends, "My child-bride is an ageless wonder." Now suddenly she saw that he hated her for this eternal youth which she tried so hard to retain. He was jealous like everyone else, didn't want her to look young. He was not her loyal admirer, happy to look years older than her.

She looked at him again, slouching on the sofa, and noticed for the first time that he had a bald patch on top of his head. Her daughter watched her silently, a tiny smile playing on her lips. They both hated her. They wanted her to age like other women, become part of the ugly army, a piece of furniture, so that people would pass by and not notice her. They wanted her to look old so that they didn't have to stand aside while she basked in the glory of youth. Her own family, the two people closest to her, were her enemies.

Malti got up and walked out of the room. It was time for her yoga but she went and lay down on her bed instead. She didn't feel like putting her eye mask on.

*

The invitations went out the next day and though neither Tutu nor Tanya had shown her a card, she knew what it said because she had seen a rough draft on the desk.

"My wife is turning fifty at last. Join us to celebrate this great occasion."

Fifty. Such a terrible number. The end of one's youth and the beginning of middle age, tedious ill health, menopause, hysterectomy, backaches and worst of all – ageing skin.

Malti woke up on her birthday and looked out of the window. It was a perfect winter morning, sparkling with golden sunshine. She felt like closing her eyes and going back to sleep again. A strange inertia crept over her. What was the point of going for a morning walk or working out or doing her painful yoga asanas – she would soon be dead, anyway. "Fifty-year-old middle aged woman dies in her bedroom," she could see the tiny black words in newsprint. "Oh, so sad but she didn't look fifty," people would say. She didn't care now what they said. Her life was over. Her face felt puffy and her hands suddenly began to tremble. Was her body protesting? Let it rot. She didn't care anymore. Her husband

and daughter hated her. Her friends were jealous of her. Was it really worth it, this young face and body? This endless hard work on the treadmill, on the cross-trainer like a pet mouse going round and round in its cage forever.

Malti lay in bed and looked at the trees. The silk-cotton was in full bloom and a tiny green bird with a red head stared back at her. She walked to the window and inhaled. A strong scent of roses drifted into her room from the garden. She peered out and saw that the veranda was filled with flowers. Tutu and Tanya were struggling with a banner which said, "Fifty, going on twenty."

Tanya began to giggle. "Shh, she'll hear us. Let her sleep," whispered Tutu.

Malti looked down at them and suddenly her heart, so heavy with sadness till a moment ago, gave a lurch and she felt a strange sensation flooding her, a sort of heaviness which came after you had eaten something delicious but fattening. She knew she was about to cry. She had never allowed herself to because it ruined your under-eye skin, but now she couldn't help it. Over the last twenty-four hours she had been through so many different and unusual emotions. It was as if the feelings she had kept in check all these years, the laughter, the sadness, the anger, the tears and the joy had suddenly bubbled up and were pouring out of her her. She tried half-heartedly to control her tears but they kept streaming down her face. Her skin would get ruined now and her eyes would be all swollen and red. At the party people would look at her in horror and say, "She's aged overnight."

*

She was fifty, but suddenly she didn't seem to care. Tutu and Tanya loved her not because she was young-looking and well-preserved with the body of a young girl, but because she was Malti. They didn't hate her because she looked young, nor did they love her because she did.

She was Tutu's wife and Tanya's mother. She meant the world to them and she had never seen it before. It had been so difficult to stay in the rat race of looking young that she had forgotten who they were, what they meant to her. It was so easy to look beyond yourself and actually see the people around you. Why hadn't she realised this before?

Malti washed her face quickly and wore her kimono wrap. Her morning ritual of papaya skin rub and almond oil forgotten, she rushed downstairs. Today she would allow herself to eat, laugh and age a little. It wasn't such a bad thing to grow a bit older on your birthday. Just a tiny bit though, like an offering to the gods to ward off the evil eye. But tomorrow ... tomorrow she would renew her battle against time. She would be the youngest sixty-year-old anyone had ever seen.